THE AUCTION MURDERS

An enthralling crime mystery full of twists

(Yorkshire Murder Mysteries Book 5)

ROGER SILVERWOOD

First published as "Mantrap"

Revised edition 2019
Joffe Books, London
www.joffebooks.com

First published as "Mantrap" 2006

**Please join our mailing list for free Kindle
crime thriller, detective, and mystery books
and new releases.**
joffebooks.com/contact
ISBN: 978-1-78931-252-2

'Little finger touching the little finger of the person sitting next to you, please,' the tiny old woman, Selina Bailey, said in a small, high-pitched voice. 'To make a circle. Palms downwards. Everybody. Thank you. That's it. Now, there are *seven* of us, and *seven* is the ideal number. Yes. So, when I switch off the light, do not break the circle, and please maintain absolute silence until I am asleep, and my control takes over. It will only take a minute or so. I must tell you that the spirits do not always come, but if they get in touch with you, please speak up quickly or the power may go and they will fade away. I hope that tonight, you all make contact with that special somebody. Your friends in the spirit world may manifest themselves as you had been used to seeing them, or maybe only part of them will appear, usually head and shoulders, or in the form of ectoplasm from me, or simply in the form of vapour. Also, a spirit may be visible to one person and not to another. You may see nothing. In fact, unless you are specially gifted, you probably will see nothing. If you do see anything, don't be afraid. It would be absolutely normal. The spirits would *never* do you any harm. One more thing, ... I may stay in a trance, faint or fall asleep, but I will awaken naturally in due course, so please leave me be ... I have done this many times. I will be perfectly all right. You will know when the spirits have gone … then, please gather up your things, leave the house and drop the latch. Now, if you are ready, absolute silence please.'

The three men and three women visitors looked expectantly round the table at each other. The lady opposite little Mrs Bailey was licking her lips and her eyes were darting in all directions. The man next to her pressed hard on her little finger with his, and smiled reassuringly. Mary Angel felt a little tremor in her stomach. Her husband, Michael Angel, an inspector in the CID, sniffed and wondered what on earth he was doing there.

'Everybody hold that position please,' Mrs Bailey said. She stood up, crossed to the lights switch by the door. The room was plunged in darkness.

Somebody gasped.

'Quiet! Please!' Mrs Bailey squawked sharply as she returned to the table and shuffled back into her seat. 'Absolute silence, please. I have a feeling this is going to be a very good night. Yes. Now, little fingers touching please. Somebody is not completing the circle … Mrs Haig? … that's it, thank you. Now absolute silence, please.'

Everything went quiet. Nobody could see a thing and all that could be heard was the rich ticking of the grandfather clock at the side of the fireplace.

After a few seconds, Angel felt Mary's finger quiver nervously against his. He pursed his lips. This sort of thing wasn't his idea of entertainment. He didn't believe in all this hocus pocus. Shuffling in his chair, he noticed his feet felt very cold; and that was odd. He recalled the saying, 'he's got cold feet', but he didn't feel afraid of anything. When you've been in the police force thirty years, there's not a lot left to be afraid of. But his feet were certainly cold and getting colder. He sniffed. He thought he could smell something sickly sweet … violets or lilies or something. The woman on his left smelled of something uncertain from a bottle. And then there was an indistinct rustle … somebody was behind him or were they in front? It was nothing. His mind was playing tricks.

Suddenly he heard deep breathing coming from across the table in the direction of Mrs Bailey. As it got louder, it was like snoring. Then it stopped and a chirpy, deep manly voice erupted from her. 'I've got a gentleman here eager to contact 'his lad', as he calls him.'

Angel wished he could see something ... anything.

Mrs Bailey in the chirpy man's voice said, 'Yes, he says his name is Ernest?'

Angel's eyebrows shot up. He heard Mary gasp. She nudged him. 'Go on,' she whispered urgently. 'Go on, Michael. Tell her. *It's your dad!*'

Angel's father's name had certainly been Ernest, but he reckoned it couldn't be him.

'Go on. Before he goes away,' Mary whispered more urgently.

'He wants to talk to his son, Michael,' the medium said. 'Is there a Michael here?'

Surely, it couldn't be *his* father, could it? He didn't like talking to someone he couldn't see. 'Er yes. It could be me ...' he heard himself saying.

'He says it's all right about Cyril Sagar. You are not to worry about it any more. He says it was *his* fault entirely. They've met up and are now bosom pals.'

Angel's jaw dropped.

'He also says your mother, Betty, and your aunt Kate are chinning away; they never stop talking. And Aunt Kate no longer needs a stick. He's fading. He's fading. He's gone.'

Mary's hand reached out for his. She held on to it tightly. Angel sighed. He sat in the dark, speechless — his mouth wide open.

*

Michael Angel drove the car home in silence. Mary's eyes were shining. She chattered animatedly about the message from her father-in-law, the reference to her husband's late, great-aunt's stick, the floor being so cold in the presence of 'spirits', and the spirit in the form of a cloud they saw in the corner of the room in front of a big vase on a pedestal, at the end of the session when the light was switched on again. The experience had had an unexpected, profound effect on her and she said so, repeatedly. Angel sat quietly and appeared to be concentrating on driving the car. She had expected an analytical and practical explanation of everything from him, but he returned only a few monosyllabic responses to her outpouring.

When they arrived home, they switched on the lights and she made herself a mug of coffee and went into the sitting-room. Angel had poured himself a small Scotch and was sitting in an armchair. 'Well, what did you think?' she asked. 'You've hardly said a word.'

He sipped the drink, pursed his lips and said, 'Yes, well …' He shrugged.

She stared at him. *'Hearing from your dad after all these years?'*

He shook his head. 'That wasn't my dad.'

'Sounded like it to me.'

He shook his head again. 'My father wouldn't have done anything wrong to anybody, and he certainly wouldn't go around telling people about it … like that.'

'Who was this Cyril Sagar anyway?'

'Dad told me about him, years ago.'

'You never mentioned him.'

'He joined the force about the same time Dad did. Goes back to the fifties. Before I was born. For years they were mates. My mother was none too happy about him; he was a drunk. I met him once or twice. He came to the house. I don't know all the details, I was only a tot, something to do with Dad trying to cover for him and it going wrong. Sagar got drummed out of the force. And later he took his own life.'

Mary shuddered. 'Oh. How?'

'They'd just finished building a stretch of the M1 near here somewhere. Sagar had had a skinful of ale, had a row with his wife and he jumped off it.'

4

'When was this?'

'Sometime in the sixties.'

'Did you ever meet his wife? I wonder what she was like.'

'No, I never did. Anyway, that wasn't my father there, talking to me. He wouldn't have brought *that* up. He would have been talking about my mother, or fishing or the garden or Superintendent Foster.'

'You don't *know* that.'

'You don't know it was him, either. You didn't know him *that* well.'

'He knew your mother's name was Betty. Did your mother and your aunt Kate have a lot in common? Your father said they never stop chinning.'

'I suppose so. I hardly remember Aunt Kate. But Dad wouldn't have used a word like 'chinning'.'

'And what's this about your aunt Kate not needing a stick?'

'I don't know. I reckon it's Mrs Bailey's vivid imagination.'

'But you had an aunt Kate?'

'Yes. Great-aunt Kate. We've photos of her somewhere with my grandad. Lived at Ackworth. She died when I was a lad. I can just remember her. Smelled of mothballs. Needed a shave.'

'Was she lame?'

'Can't remember.'

'Well, if she had a gammy leg, it's now healed!'

'If you like,' he said patiently. 'But her gammy leg is in a box six foot down in Mawdsley cemetery. I shouldn't think it's any better today than when it was put down there with the rest of her forty years ago.'

'*Oh*!' she replied impatiently. 'You don't believe in *any*thing.'

'I do. I do. There's more in the universe than we'll ever understand, but I don't believe there are any explanations to be found from Mrs Bailey.'

'She seemed honest enough. Straightforward. No dramatics. What about that spirit just disappearing as the light went on. You said you saw it. How do you explain *that*? I think most people there saw it. Mrs Haig said she saw a woman's face in it. Her husband saw it too.'

He nodded and wiped his hand across his face. 'Yes. I did see it. Like a cloud. I didn't see any faces though.'

'The light would frighten the spirit away, I suppose. You admit there was something? You admit Mrs Bailey isn't a fraud then?'

'No. I don't admit anything of the sort.'

'But you can't explain away the spirit in the corner dissolving right in front of your eyes, can you?' Mary said stubbornly.

Angel's jaw stiffened. 'It was only … er, a sort of mist.' He shook his head irritably and stood up. 'Mary, I'm going to bed,' he announced.

She smiled. She knew he would have stayed and argued if he had been certain of his facts. She felt she had won a minor battle.

He turned to go into the kitchen.

'Just a minute, love,' she called. 'You've some fluff or something on the back of your jacket.'

He stopped in the doorway and waited. She came over and picked it off. 'Oh,' she said, her eyes glowing. 'Oh,' she added excitedly, her eyes and mouth opening wide. 'Look at that.' She held the item safely cupped in both hands. 'Do you know what that is, Michael?'

He peered into her hands and said, 'Yes. A little white feather.'

'Do you know what it *means*?' she said earnestly, her eyes shining.

'No,' he said, stifling a yawn.

'It means we've been in the presence of angels!'

*

The smiling, brassy-faced auctioneer brought the gavel down triumphantly. 'Sold to Mr Enderby for £110. Thank you, sir. Thank you. Now the next sixty lots, ladies and gentlemen, are sold on the instruction of Her Majesty's Customs and Excise following the untimely death of Lord Archibald Ogmore. The first lot then is lot number 121: silver teapot, sugar and milk. Weight 62 ounces. Assayed in London in 1841. Reputed to have been used originally by Queen Victoria at Windsor Castle and given by her and Prince Albert to Lord Arthur and Lady Alice Ogmore on the occasion of their marriage in 1842. Was in regular use in Ogmore Hall until a short time ago. Has been repaired ... still, highly desirable. Who will start me off at two thousand pounds? ... A thousand pounds then? ... Well, five hundred?'

The big white-haired lady in the front row waved her purple pot-handled walking stick and said, 'Two hundred and fifty pounds.'

'Ah.' He sniffed. 'Thank you, Mrs Buller-Price. That's a start anyway.' He surveyed the room. 'Three hundred anywhere?'

A hand waved at the back of the room. 'Thank you, sir. Three hundred.'

The auctioneer peered expectantly at Mrs Buller-Price.

She pursed her lips and then said, 'Three hundred and twenty pounds.'

'Three hundred and twenty,' he announced and looked to the back of the room. 'Three hundred and forty? ... No? All done. I'm selling.' He brought the gavel down with a flourish. 'Sold to Mrs Buller-Price for three hundred and twenty pounds. Thank you, madam. The next lot is lot 122. Pair of brass candlesticks.'

She nodded, smiled, leaned on her stick and stood up. Her mountainous size filled out the grey waterproof raincoat like a barrage balloon. She shuffled through the side aisle to the cashier's office, where she stood in line behind two people. Eventually she reached the counter, paid the money and collected the tea service, then made her way out through the swing doors, across the crowded car park to her 1986 Bentley. She unlocked the boot and was stowing the tea set safely, when a tall man in a light-coloured raincoat approached her from behind.

'Mrs Buller-Price?' he said in an educated voice.

She turned round to face him. 'Yes.'

'You've just bought that tea service?'

'Yes.'

'It's badly knocked about, you know.'

'I had noticed,' she said smiling. 'It wouldn't have gone so cheaply if it had been in perfect condition.'

'The teapot has been repaired.'

'Yes, but each piece is hallmarked silver, and if it *was* used by Queen Victoria, it has quite a provenance.'

He smiled. 'Oh I'm sure that it was used by her. Are you a dealer?'

'Good gracious, no. What's your interest, young man?'

'I've poured many a gallon of tea out of that pot, madam. Let me introduce myself. My name is Sanson. Geoffrey Sanson. I was butler to Lord and Lady Ogmore. That teapot is an old friend of mine.'

Mrs Buller-Price smiled. 'Really? How interesting!'

A limousine glided up noiselessly next to the Bentley.

Sanson glanced at it and then turned quickly away. 'I must go,' he muttered.

He scuttled off, darting between other people loading their cars, and was soon out of sight.

Two well-fed men with ponytails slid quickly out of the cream leather seats of the limo. They slammed the doors and, fastening the middle button of their double-breasted Savile Row suits, rushed off in a cloud of cigar smoke in the direction of the saleroom doors.

She stood for a few seconds and watched them go, then turned and climbed laboriously into the Bentley.

Another car raced into the car park. It was an open-topped white sports job driven by a fair-haired glamour piece in her thirties. She was wearing a tight-fitting powder-blue top and trousers. Mrs Buller-Price peered over the steering wheel; she thought the outfit inappropriate: more suitable for a nightclub or the theatre or even the bedroom. At first, she didn't recognize the slim young woman. Then it came to her. 'Of course, Lady Ogmore!' she muttered. The young beauty, who had recently been widowed.

The woman ran in high heels to the saleroom doors, pulled one open and dashed inside.

At the same time the two men with the ponytails appeared from the auction room. They were coming towards Mrs Buller-Price in a hurry.

She tried not to let them notice her and fiddled unnecessarily with the dashboard controls and then her hat as one of them walked up the side of her car. She noticed he had a red gold signet ring on his pinky and both sported the new fashion of designer facial hair, favoured by ageing gigolos and fading football stars.

The men were soon in the car. It reversed into the aisle, then on to the main road and left towards Bromersley town centre.

She was about to start her car when she saw the woman in blue, Lady Ogmore, come out of the saleroom. She saw her run to the white sports car and belt off in the same direction.

Then suddenly a torrent of people — a hundred or more, their eyes shining and mouths open — poured through the double doors, arms in the air, flooding across the car park while making for the main street or their cars.

Her jaw dropped. She got out of her car and stood holding the door. A woman was rushing past. She called out to her, 'What's the matter? Is there a fire?'

'Don't go in there,' she screamed, her eyes like saucers. 'A man has just been stabbed.'

'Stabbed? Oh. Oh dear,' she said. Her Adam's apple bounced twice. 'Then I *must* go in. See what I can do. I'm a qualified nurse.'

'Too late. He's dead. He's been murdered!' she wailed and ran off.

2

Three days after DI Angel had attended the seance with his wife, and two days after he had assisted DS Gawber and DC Scrivens to arrest four men in the local three star hotel, The Feathers, where he had in the fracas received an injury from a boot and had needed a surgical operation on his knee, Angel, with the aid of aluminium elbow crutches, shuffled out of the chief constable's office.

He was not in the best of moods.

The chiefs secretary closed the door behind him, which was as well; if he hadn't been hindered by the crutches, he might have been tempted to slam it. He stumped down the station steps, as quietly as his temper and his desire to remain in employment as a policeman would allow. Descending them one at a time, at the bottom he swung towards the CID room and hobbled up to the door. He peered round the jamb. There were four plainclothes men viewing photographs on a computer.

'Anybody seen DS Gawber or DS Crisp?' he growled.

'No sir.'

'Cadet Ahaz?' he enquired.

A voice from behind him said, 'I'm here, sir.'

He turned round: a three-point turn was tricky with crutches.

Cadet Ahmed Ahaz was a 20-year-old Indian, who was immaculately turned out in a well-pressed dark suit. He had small teeth and big bright eyes. His jet-black hair was brushed straight back and shone brighter than the chief constable's Mercedes. His speech was clipped but always distinct.

'What you doing, creeping about like that, lad? Who do you think you are? Uriah Heep?'

Ahmed straightened up, his eyes flashed, he breathed in deeply, stuck out his small chest and said, 'I'm not *creeping* about, sir.'

'You're taking advantage of me, because I'm dependent on these damned sticks,' he said, waving a crutch at him.

'No, sir,' Ahmed protested.

Angel took a step towards him and leaned forward until he was three inches from his face. 'Well listen up. Listen up good. And keep this to yourself. I want you to go down to the cellar and find the personnel files going back to 1950, and look up a PC Cyril Sagar. He was a constable here from about then until 1962 or '63, when he took his own life. Now I want to know all that is recorded about him. Got it?'

'Yes sir.'

'Right. Crack on with it then, lad.'

'One moment please, sir.'

Angel's face went scarlet. 'Now!' he bellowed.

'No sir. I have to tell you something. It's very important, but you don't give me a chance. The super wants you now, sir, and he said it was very urgent.'

'What?' he roared. He turned away and started rocking down the corridor. 'Why didn't you tell me straightaway instead of acting like Jonathan Dimbleby ... giving me a load of smart-arse crosstalk?'

Ahmed shook his head slowly.

'Find Gawber and send him to my office, pronto!' Angel added without looking back.

The cadet watched him go, admiring the speed the big man was making on his crutches.

'Right, sir,' he called.

Angel rocked the crutches down the green corridor to the office at the end of the line. The door had a white plastic panel with the words 'DETECTIVE SUPERINTENDENT H. HARKER' painted on it. He tapped on the door with the butt of a crutch.

'Come in.'

A big man with a head shaped like a turnip and covered with short white hair focused his bloodshot eyes on him from behind a desk. He always wore a pained expression and looked as if he had just swallowed a bag of nails. 'You wanted me, sir?' Angel said.

'Sit down. Been hunting you all over,' he snarled, and stuck a finger in the corner of his mouth, to remove an irritating nail lodged between his teeth.

Angel took the seat and laid the crutches on the floor. 'I was stuck with the chief.'

Harker sniffed disinterestedly, pointed at the crutches and said, 'How long are you going to be dependent on those damned things?'

'Doctor said a couple of weeks or so.'

'Don't want to give you something you can't manage. And if working makes it worse, you had better stop at home.'

Angel shook his head. 'No.'

'You could take your summer holidays?'

Angel didn't like the sound of that. 'This happened in the course of work, sir. I want to be fit enough to *enjoy* my summer holidays, thank you.'

The superintendent smiled, which was very unusual. It was rumoured around Bromersley station that every time he smiled, a donkey died.

'A man's been stabbed at Snatchpole's, the auctioneers. Was taken to Bromersley General but he was DOA. Came in at 1504. I've sent Mac, SOCO and two PCs.'

'Right, sir,' he said and reached down for the crutches. He took his leave and charged up the green corridor. He could move fast on these crutches if the way ahead was clear.

As he took the bend, he saw Ahmed and DS Gawber waiting outside his office.

'Ah Ron,' he boomed. 'Take me to Snatchpole's, auctioneers, on Doncaster Road.'

Gawber nodded.

'And Ahmed, find out all you can about Snatchpole's. See if there's anything known on the NPC. And find out what the hell Crisp is up to. I can never find that lad when I want him. Try his mobile. I want him at Snatchpole's, *now*. And I want Scrivens there as well. Well, go on, then. Get on with it.'

*

Gawber pulled up on the auctioneer's car park. The only other vehicles there were a police car, the SOCOs' van and Dr Mac's car.

Angel surveyed the scene and sniffed. They made their way through the double doors into the saleroom. Two uniformed constables were chatting to each other at the foot of the podium. When they saw Angel, they separated and straightened up. Two SOCOs in white paper suits, hats and rubber boots were on their hands and knees at the back of the room. One had a brush with aluminium powder on it tickling the wood panelling, the other was gazing studiously at the carpet. Seated at the side of the room was the auctioneer, perspiring and wiping his face with a big white handkerchief. He stood up and looked enquiringly across at the new arrivals.

'Afternoon. I'm Detective Inspector Angel. Who are you?'

'James Snatchpole. I'm the proprietor of this business,' he said evenly.

'A man was killed here this afternoon, sir. Did you see what happened?'

Gawber took out his notebook and made notes as the interview progressed.

'Yes. I was up there, on the podium, selling surplus effects from the Ogmore estate. It was going very well. I had reached lot 190, that beautiful oil painting of the original house at Littlecombe. And I drew the attention of the sale-room to it, when there was a gasp from somewhere at the back of the hall. A tall man in a grey suit, who was standing leaning against the wall, bent forward and then sort of rolled out of sight on to the floor. A few other customers near him also noticed. There was a bit of confusion, several went to assist him, then a woman screamed, there were a few gasps, then someone said he'd been stabbed, and another said he was dead. I saw Dr Sinclair on the front row there, and I asked him to take a look, see what he could do for the poor man. He looked at him and said a dagger had gone into his chest and that he was dead and that I should phone for the police, which I did. The customers were upset when they saw the man and the blood. I think they were afraid. I'm not really surprised. After all, it certainly looked like murder, and under their noses so to speak. Then everybody made a beeline for the door. I've never had anything like this before.'

'Yes,' Angel said heavily. 'Thank you. Do you know who the dead man is?'

'No.'

'Was there anybody standing near to him?'

'Oh yes. There were lots of people. The room was crowded. The Ogmore sale had brought a lot of local people, as well as dealers from different parts of the country. He was surrounded. The room was chock-a-block.'

'Did this chap buy anything? Or bid for anything?'

'No. I remember the face of everyone who bids. I shall have a lot of sorting out to do. After the room emptied, I told my staff — I only have three part-timers — they might as well go home too.'

'I shall want to speak to them. And your customers?'

'I can make a list of all those who actually bought any-thing, inspector. I might recall some of the bidders, but there were a lot of faces and sightseers I didn't know.'

'Hmmm. Well, we can start there. Will you begin preparing that now? Make it as comprehensive as you can, Mr Snatchpole. Give it to my sergeant.' He nodded towards Gawber. 'We need to speak to everybody who was in the hall. Somebody must have seen something. Ron, we must ask everyone we interview who they remember seeing there.'

Gawber nodded.

Angel sighed. 'Right Mr Snatchpole. Thanks very much.'

Suddenly there was a noise behind them. Angel turned to see the doors opening and the tall, handsome figure of DS Crisp coming in, followed by a younger, lanky lad, DC Scrivens.

Angel's eyebrows lifted. 'Where the hell have you two been?'

Crisp opened his mouth to reply but Angel said, 'Never mind. It's bound to be something I can't check up on!' He turned to Gawber. 'Fill them in, Ron.'

Then he crossed over to the elder of the two SOCOs in the white forensic paper overalls. 'What you got, Mac?'

The white-haired Glaswegian looked up. 'Not much. Blood and more blood, all, almost certainly, from the victim, and a million fingerprints.'

'What about the body?'

'I've yet to see it. It was whisked off to A and E. DOA, I was told. I understand it's male. A wound in the chest cavity.'

'Any ID?'

'Not yet. We're about finished here; there's nothing else. I'll make a superficial examination when I get back and give you a ring.'

'Hmmm. Thanks, Mac.'

Angel turned to the three detectives. 'Crisp, you'd better nip along and see if anybody in the bank next door saw anything, and then get started on Snatchpole's list. Scrivens, have a word in that baker's shop, then see as many as you can. Tackle them while their memories are still fresh. Those you don't see today, carry on with them first thing in the morning.'

They bustled off.

He turned to Gawber. 'Pick me up at home, first thing, Ron. I'll cadge a lift back to the station with Mac now.'

Ten minutes later, the doctor's car stopped outside the front of Bromersley police station. Angel struggled out of it, up the steps to the top and manoeuvred his way through the heavy glass door into the reception area.

A big woman with her back to him was staring at a poster on the wall; he immediately recognized the mountainous figure of Mrs Buller-Price. He sighed and pulled a face.

She heard the door slam and turned round to see who had entered. 'Ah, there you are, Inspector Angel,' she said brandishing her purple pot-knobbed walking stick. 'I have been waiting for you.'

'Oh?' His face showed he wasn't best pleased. He knew the old lady very well indeed: he considered her quite delightful, always polite, kind, generous and hospitable, but rather too much for him at that moment.

She saw his expression. 'Oh, don't look at me like that, inspector. I'm here to *help* you. And while I've been waiting, I've been looking at this wanted poster. Look.' She pointed a finger as thick as a truncheon at the photograph of a heavy-set thug. 'Him!' she said. 'I *know* him.'

Angel blinked. He glanced at it. He remembered the man was in his twenties and wanted for a particularly gruesome murder. This would be quite a coup. 'Oh,' he said. 'Where have you seen him?'

'In the tripe shop. Here, in town, in the market. Yes. That's him. He needed a shave ... and a haircut. And his fingernails needed attention!' She pointed at the photograph again. 'Yes. It's him. Quite definitely!'

Angel stared at the poster and then at Mrs Buller-Price. 'When did you last see him?' he asked urgently.

'Erm ... let me see. It would have been 1946 or 1947.'

Angel blew out a lungful of air. 'It wouldn't have been him, Mrs Buller-Price. He wasn't *born* then!'

'Oh. Oh,' she said disappointed. 'Well it looks just like him. Must be his double. I must say,' she muttered.

Angel wrinkled his nose and repositioned the crutches under his arms. His leg was aching. 'I must sit down,' he growled. 'Now was there anything else?'

'Yes. Oh yes. I was at Snatchpole's auction this afternoon where a man was murdered. I expect you know about it. And I thought I should report what I saw.'

Angel's eyebrows shot up. It was very public-spirited of her, and quite typical. 'Oh? Yes. You'd better come down to my office, then. I *must* sit down.'

'You poor man. Yes. I'll open the door for you. Is it very painful, inspector? I was a nurse in the Queen Alexandra's, you know. I know about pain. I have a certificate in trauma limitation.'

Angel took off at speed down the green corridor; she kept up with him.

They reached his office. Mrs Buller-Price opened the door, Angel pushed in, turned, flopped in the chair and dumped the crutches on the floor. 'Thank you. Aaaah. Oh that's better! Please sit down.'

She dropped her big leather bag on the floor, lowered her stick carefully and looked round the room. 'Very nice,' she said easing herself into the chair. 'Very nice. Restful. I like this room. Yes. Do you know, it has the same colour scheme as Margaret Thatcher's dressing-room.'

Angel blinked then shook his head. 'It's just an office, Mrs Buller-Price. Now, you were at Snatchpole's auction this afternoon, you were saying?'

'Oh yes. A very interesting sale,' she said, shaking her four chins energetically. 'He was selling some oddments from Ogmore Hall.'

'And what did you see?'

'Oh?' she beamed. Her hands went up excitedly. 'I bought the most delightful old silver teapot, with sugar and milk. Sometime in the possession of Queen Victoria. Hallmarked 1841. A bit knocked about and soldered in two

17

places, but still very much the style of extravagance of the time. It's a joy to look at, hold and feel. I shall very much enjoy drinking tea from *that*! And you will too, when next you come up to Tunistone. I shall not use it until you come. You must come and we will christen it together.'

He shook his head impatiently. 'Yes. Thank you. I meant did you see anything of the murder?'

'Oh no. No. I was in the car park at the critical time, I believe. But I did see two strange men with ponytails rushing by me … *first* out of the saleroom, after the murder, I shouldn't wonder.'

'Oh? Really? Ponytails are becoming quite common these days, aren't they?'

She shook her head disapprovingly. 'Not for men. Not for men in their fifties or sixties.' Angel nodded passively. 'Mmm. Anything else strange about them?'

'Yes. They both had facial hair, trimmed in some sort of geometric pattern, like footballers and certain peculiar people now appearing on our television screens.'

'Anything else? Did you see anybody you knew?'

'Hmm. I saw dear old Doctor Sinclair. And I saw Lady Emerald Ogmore in a smart open-top car … in a striking blue outfit … no doubt checking on how the sale was going. Hmmm. Pity about her husband, dying so young.'

'Hmm.'

'Leaving her so poor.'

'Poor?' he blinked.

'Well, relatively poor. She's moved out of Ogmore Hall, you know. She's in a little bungalow on the estate. It was built for their housekeeper a few years ago. Bit of a comedown. But it'll afford her good, safe shelter. I expect Ogmore Hall will have to be sold.'

Angel leaned back in the chair and stretched out the plastered leg under the kneehole of the desk. He pulled faces, sighed and then beamed. 'She's got the Ogmore diamonds, hasn't she? Worth millions.'

'It's one diamond, inspector. But it's a beauty. And nobody is saying who has that.' 'She'll have inherited it, won't she? There's nobody else.'

'Unless it's been sold.'

'Who knows? Archie Ogmore *was* a bit wild. Not like his father.'

Mrs Buller-Price's bright eyes shone brighter. 'But *just* like his grandfather! I was once on a hunt when Lionel Ogmore was host, and I was acting MFH, and I can tell you, inspector, it wasn't only a fox he was after!'

Angel smiled.

The phone rang.

'Excuse me.' He reached over for the handset. 'Angel.'

'It's Mac.'

'Ah yes, Mac,' he said eagerly, reaching out for a pen. 'What you got?'

'The name of the dead man is Sanson, Geoffrey Sanson.'

Angel began to scribble on an envelope. 'That's clever of you.'

'His driving licence was in his wallet in his pocket. He's aged fifty. Died instantly from the piercing of his heart by a three-sided, eight-inch blade. It was still in him. Has several fresh bruises to the stomach, delivered before the stabbing. He was butler to the Ogmores. One of the porters here recognized him. He's a neighbour.'

'Ah. Thanks very much, Mac.'

'We're going straight up there. The address is 22 Branscombe Avenue.'

'Got it. Thanks, Mac. See you there in about five minutes.' He replaced the phone thoughtfully and looked across at Mrs Buller-Price. 'Sorry about that interruption. Hmm.' He suddenly looked very sombre. 'I'm very sorry. I have to go.'

He reached out for the phone again and pressed a button.

A voice answered, 'Cadet Ahaz.'

'Ahmed … Come in here, lad, pronto.' He replaced the phone.

'Sorry to bustle you off like this, Mrs Buller-Price.'

She found her bag and stick and was making for the door. 'I have to go anyway.' She turned back at the door. 'It's been a delight to see you again, inspector, as always.'

He smiled. 'And you, Mrs Buller-Price. Thank you for your help.'

'Pop in for tea sometime. I always have a cup of tea and a fairy cake about half past three. We will try out the new teapot. You're always welcome.'

'Thank you.'

There was a knock at the door.

'Come in.'

It was Ahmed.

'Show Mrs Buller-Price to her car, lad, and then come back here smartish.'

They went out.

Angel reached over for the phone and pressed a button. 'Traffic division.'

'Yes.'

'Angel here. I need to get to Branscombe Avenue.'

'We'll find you something, sir. In two or three minutes … at the front.'

Ten minutes later, a Range Rover from traffic division delivered Angel at the small, semi-detached house in a quiet part of the suburbs of Bromersley. An unmarked car was parked outside as well as the SOCOs' van. Angel propelled himself up the path and arrived at the front door. He banged the knocker and the door was opened by Dr Mac in his forensic whites.

'Come in, Michael.'

'What you found?'

Dr Mac's bushy eyebrows shot upwards. 'It's a mess,' he said, pulling open the door. 'The place has been broken into. There's a window at the back smashed. The next-door neighbour says it must have been done while she was at the shops, about four o'clock.'

Angel positioned the crutches on the doormat and launched himself up the step. He sniffed. 'This break-in would be after he was murdered then?'

'Looks like it.'

Angel pushed himself out of the hall into the drawing room. What a sight. The doctor had not been exaggerating. The floor of the room was a mass of newspapers, some green and some conventional black and white strewn everywhere. There were also books scattered about … sofa cushions had been pulled out and some chairs were upside down. The sideboard drawers too had been pulled out, the contents tipped on to the floor while the drawers were piled roughly in a corner. The other rooms had been similarly and savagely turned over.

Angel sniffed. 'A pretty thorough job. By an amateur.'

'Aye.'

'Wonder what he was looking for?'

Mac shrugged.

Angel sighed. 'Any dabs?'

'The dead man's, I expect. I will check, of course. Nothing fresh.'

'Any footprints, drugs, cash, porn, firearms, gold?'

'No. Only racing papers, tip sheets and betting slips.'

'Did you see a bookie's name on any of that rubbish?'

'No.'

'Or a cheque book, or cheque book stubs?'

'No.'

Angel sniffed and banged the crutches impatiently. 'You're not much help are you?'

Mac glared at him and dropped down on his knees. 'Neither are you. You've just stabbed my bag and broken my rectal thermometer!'

21

3

The following morning, Ahmed was hovering near Angel's office, and when the inspector arrived, he followed him into the room with a sheet of A4 in his hand.

'What you got there, lad?' Angel said. 'Your last will and testament?'

'No sir.'

'What have we got on Snatchpole, then?' he asked as he threw his coat at him. Ahmed caught it and hung it on a hook at the side of a stationery cupboard.

'Nothing, sir. Clean as a whistle.'

'Oh,' Angel grunted. He sat down at the desk and began to finger through the post. He looked up irritably. 'Well, lad, what is that bit of paper you keep waving about? Is it your P45?'

'No sir,' Ahmed said firmly and grinned. 'It's that info you wanted on PC Sagar. Didn't know how quickly you wanted it. I've got all there is in the personnel file from 1950 to 1962. These are my rough notes,' he said waving the paper. 'I can soon tap it into the computer and let you have a legible copy, if you like.'

'No lad. Just let me have a look,' he said holding out his hand.

'You won't be able to read my writing, sir.'

Angel blew out an impatient sigh. 'Well then, read it to me. *Read* it.'

Ahmed nodded. 'Well, sir, the first mention of Cyril Sagar on the station strength was as a PC in 1950, when he was eighteen years of age.'

'That'd be when he first joined the force.'

'It said that, at first, he served as a clerk. His conduct and service were excellent as recorded by the then Chief Constable Whyke. He went on a short course to Hendon and came back with passes and a commendation. In 1953, he went into traffic and, in the same year, got the job escorting the Queen's car through the borough when she visited the town shortly after her coronation, and he got a service ribbon award for it. Then … he got his annual increments in pay … nothing unusual recorded … then nothing, sir. Just entries on the payroll and the quarterly strength figures for *nine* years.'

Angel sniffed. 'That's how it is, lad. You are best not expecting anything exciting, being a copper. It's the South Yorkshire police, not *Top of the Pops*.'

'There was nothing at all about him through to 1962, when he was disciplined for being absent without notice for three days in April and then again in July for a week. There was no further mention of him after the end of July in 1962. That must have been when he killed himself, sir. There was mention of a gift to his widow of £200 in August, which was collected by subscription from his fellow workmates. There was no record of a pension, so I suppose his widow didn't get one. And that's all there was.'

Angel nodded slowly. 'Aye. Right, lad. That's *just* what I wanted to know. Now tear it up.'

Ahmed's jaw dropped. 'What? Tear it up, sir?'

'Yes,' he said. He massaged his earlobe between finger and thumb and added, 'And forget all about it.'

Ahmed blinked. 'Right, sir.' He looked at him briefly, then proceeded to tear the page vigorously and tossed the fragments into the waste bin.

Angel had the essential facts about Cyril Sagar. They had confirmed what he remembered his father had told him of the sorry saga.

'Now I want you to get the phone book and see how many Sagars there are. There won't be many. Check them off against the electoral roll. I'm looking for a woman aged between about sixty-six and seventy-eight. See how many you get.'

'Right, sir.'

Angel rubbed his chin. 'Too much to do and not enough hands,' he muttered. He wanted to be interviewing some of the people present at that auction room the previous afternoon. He felt certain there would be a witness; surely somebody saw something. He turned back to Ahmed. 'See if you can find Sanson's next of kin. And ring 'traffic' and ask them to organize a lift for me to Lady Ogmore's. I'm going up in the world,' he sniffed.

*

Angel struggled up the corridor, through reception, out of the front door and down the stone steps. Right on cue, an unmarked car pulled up at the front of the station and a man leaned out of the window. 'Inspector Angel?'

'Yes.'

'Lady Ogmore's place, sir?'

'Aye.'

The young officer in plain clothes helped him into the car and then drove along Bradford Road towards Huddersfield. About two miles out of town, where Bromersley Road joined the main Huddersfield to Barnsley road there was an island roundabout; in the centre of it, was an imposing fountain surrounded by long-stemmed flowers. Water gushed from a spout in a tall pillar and dribbled graciously down a run of small marble steps into a contained pool below. Around the top of the pillar were four stone-carved plaques each facing a point of the compass; on each plaque was the Ogmore coat of arms, consisting of a lion's head, and underneath that, a long sword with a snake twined around it; below that was a commemorative inscription that read: 'This fountain has been generously donated to the town of Bromersley by Lord Arthur and Lady Alice Ogmore to commemorate sixty glorious years of Queen Victoria's reign. July 21st 1897.'

The car slowed, drove round the fountain, and took the second exit off it on to Huddersfield Road and alongside the high wall of the Ogmore estate. A hundred yards along were big black gates. The car drove through them to a smart little bungalow sited just inside, on the edge of the estate, several hundred yards from the big house itself.

Angel opened the car door and heaved himself out. He balanced on one foot while he pulled out the crutches and placed them under his arms. 'Thank you, lad,' he called through the car window. 'Just hang on a minute, will you? Make sure somebody's in.'

He hopped to the little white gate, opened it, rocked on the crutches four paces to the front door, lifted the knocker and hammered it. It was a full minute before he heard the sliding of a bolt and the rattle of keys; the door opened to reveal a slim woman with a big tousle of fair hair, scarlet lips and a voluminous blue housecoat that smothered her and seemed big enough to be wrapped round her several times. One of her slim white hands shakily held a cigarette, the other clasped the silk robe close to her chest. She was strikingly beautiful, with a very small head and a delicate face with high cheeks tapering down to her chin, and fair skin that had not been spoiled with years of cheap cosmetics. Her lips, however, were savagely made up in scarlet in the shape of a W. The backs of her hands showed the ligaments and bones and traces of veins, accentuating how slight she was. Her small pink nails reflected in the light.

She peered at him through half-closed eyes and pushed a hanging strand of hair out of the way. 'Yes,' she drawled in a low key. 'What is it?'

'Detective Inspector Angel, Bromersley CID. Are you Lady Ogmore?'

'I think so,' she said drowsily. 'Yes, of course.' She suddenly put a hand to her forehead, smiled and then moaned. Then she added, 'Come along in. I've been expecting you. It's about dear old Sanson isn't it? Better get it over with.' She pulled open the door and stood back.

'Thank you,' Angel said. He waved an acknowledgement to the driver of the police car and turned back to the door.

The police car drove off.

The woman watched him manoeuvre the crutches through the narrow opening and swing himself into the room. She looked down at his leg and said, 'Have you been skiing?'

He smiled. 'Just a misunderstanding with a drunk, that's all.'

'Story of my life,' she said without thinking, then she brushed past him and closed the door.

Her perfume brought back memories of a luxurious bathroom in a Parisian hotel he had stayed at for one night on a touring holiday twenty years ago.

'Sit there,' she said, pointing to a Louis XVII chair that had seen better days. She leaned over the back of it and snatched up a heavy magazine from the seat and plumped the cushion. Angel observed the title was *Models USA*; on the front cover was a photograph of a skinny girl wearing a garment made from a yard of dental floss. She threw the magazine on to the ornate, gilt marble-topped table in the centre of the room, which already held an assortment of other similar titles, plus a bottle of nail varnish, a drum of Stayput hairspray, an open pot of Helena Rubinstein cold cream, an ashtray overflowing with cigarette ends, an empty stocking packet in a torn cellophane wrapper and a dirty coffee cup.

Angel squeezed through the furniture to the chair, sat down, placed the crutches across his lap and looked round the little room.

'It's not Buckingham Palace,' she volunteered, yawning again. 'But it's home, and it's mine,' she said waving a hand in a grand gesture, though she quickly brought it back to hold the housecoat tight.

Angel smiled up at her and said, 'It's fine. It's fine.'

'Well, you can't get the staff, can you,' she muttered, smiled dreamily and took a drag on the cigarette. She looked round the room for something, but didn't seem to be able to find it. Then she shrugged and looked down at Angel. 'If you can drink coffee without sugar and milk, I'll get some. I don't have sugar or milk in the house.'

'If it's no trouble, that would be very nice. Thank you.'

'Won't take a minute,' she said and glided out through a door behind him.

Angel adjusted the cushion and sat back in the comfortable chair. It was a bright and airy little room, but crammed mercilessly full of furniture — mostly cream and gilt — which sat incongruously in front of the small, modern cream-tiled fireplace. On its ledges were pieces of Meissen, ivory and other ornaments, interspersed with letters, nail scissors, Lypsol, papers, envelopes, a box of paracetamol tablets, lipstick, postcards, opened packets of cigarettes and boxes of matches filling up every square centimetre. A waste basket at the side of the fireplace was overflowing with screwed-up paper, newspapers and empty cigarette packets. On the walls were thirty or forty gilt-framed photographs of her in some glamorous dress and jewellery. She was usually portrayed with her late husband, with British and foreign royalty, film and television celebrities or politicians. The photographs were assembled higgledy-piggledy in no particular order or symmetry.

She came back carrying two gilt and purple Crown Devon cups, and placed one of them uncertainly on the table, making another ring mark. 'Can you reach that, inspector? Do you know I have a beautiful silver salver somewhere but I can't find the bloody thing.'

Angel smiled politely. 'Thank you. Not to worry.' He leaned over for the cup, took a sip. It was not very warm. He pulled a face and put the cup down.

She slid into the chair next to him, wrapped the coat tightly round her, sipped the coffee and took a drag on a cigarette. 'You want to ask me about dear Sanson, don't you?' she said, biting her bottom lip and looking down at the carpet.

Angel nodded. He noticed the child-size foot with pink toenails and pretty ankle bone protruding through the straps of a delicate silver evening sandal.

'He was murdered, wasn't he?'

'Yes.'

'How?'

'Stabbed, we think. The post-mortem report's not in yet.'

She shuddered and pulled the housecoat higher up her neck. She took a drag from the cigarette in a staccato manner and said, 'What do you want to know? He was a lovely man. My husband and I thought the world of him, you know. He served my late father-in-law until he died, and then Archie and I moved into the Hall and we inherited him with the house. He looked after us absolutely wonderfully. Archie died a year ago. Sanson attended me for those difficult six months, until I moved here in January. He would still be looking after me, but, well, there just isn't the room, or the work. Anyway, people would have gotten the wrong idea.'

Angel nodded. 'Have you any idea who would have wanted him dead?'

She pushed the hair out of her eye. 'Nobody. Nobody. He was a real gentleman. And I *know*. I've met all sorts! He was a wonderful man. He *anticipated* everything. He *saw* to everything. I never had to worry about the running of the house. And he never intruded. He respected the intimacies of the family. He didn't tittle-tattle in the town. I can't imagine he had *any* enemies. Everybody liked him. He got on with everybody. He was great with the staff. His only vice was the telephone. He was never off it. Archie always shut a blind eye to it, but it was very inconvenient if you wanted to make a call.'

'Talking to his family?'

'No. He didn't have any family. Well, not that I know of. No, he was talking to his bookie, I believe. He was mad about the gee-gees. Had a system. Apparently made a small fortune.'

Angel wondered about that. 'Who was his bookie?'

She pursed her beautiful scarlet lips. 'Oh, I've no idea.'

'Somebody local?'

'I don't know,' she said drawing hard on the cigarette. She waved it towards him. 'I'll tell you who *would* know, if it matters. Mrs Drabble. Yes, Alison Drabble. She was our housekeeper. There's nothing she *doesn't* know. I've got her address somewhere.'

She jumped to her feet and, clutching the housecoat, her eyes panned across the mantelpiece, the window bottom and then the table. Her mouth opened.

Angel said, 'Everything all right?'

'My address book. The damned thing is here some-where,' she said, then her face brightened. 'Ah. Of course. My handbag.' She crossed to the door. 'Won't be a tick,' she said and glided out into the kitchen.

Angel frowned. He drummed his fingers on the chair arm; he took the opportunity to look up at the wall of pho-tographs. One in particular took his eye. It showed two men standing on either side of the woman behind a pedestal with a glass holder on it supporting a diamond. The photogra-pher had caught the stone emitting a beautiful spectrum of coloured light rays in three directions. The caption read: 'Lord and Lady Ogmore with Sir James Joshua, Chairman of the Diamond and Gemstone Exhibition, at Earl's Court, London, 2000, and the Ogmore Diamond, which is on show until the close of the event on Saturday.'

Another framed photograph had obviously been taken much earlier. It was of the same, strikingly beautiful woman with her hair up and wearing a low-cut white dress. That cap-tion read: 'Emerald Henderson, Oscar nominee best actress in *Romeo and Juliet*, Stratford-Upon-Avon. September 1988.' Angel heard her coming back. 'It wasn't in my handbag at all. It was on the work place thingie in the kitchen.'

As she slid into the chair and opened the book, several small photographs, newspaper cuttings, business cards and till roll receipts fell out and drifted on to the carpet. 'Oh *budgerigar*!' she fumed. She leaned forward, picked them up and stuffed them roughly in between the pages. Then she thought for a moment, riffled back through the bits and selected a business card from the little bundle and gave it to him. 'You may as well have that, Mr Angel. It's got my new telephone number on it. You might need it to get in touch.'

He reached out, glanced at it and pushed it in his pocket. 'Thank you.'

'That address. I've got it. I've got it. It's Mrs Alison Drabble, flat 24, Carlton Road, the Sanderson estate.'

Angel noted it in his leather-backed notebook. 'Thank you. Did you have any other staff at the Hall?'

'Yes. My husband had a secretary, Kate Cumberland. I haven't got her address, inspector. I have no idea where she might be,' she said and tossed the book on to the table, leaned back in the chair and took another drag at the cigarette.

He noted the name in his book. 'Can you describe her?'

She shrugged. 'Average height and weight. Dark hair. Age about thirty-five.'

Angel nodded. 'Anybody else?'

'No. We didn't have gardeners anymore: the grounds were maintained by contractors from Leeds. We had the odd bit of extra kitchen help and serving when we had a dinner party. Sanson used to see to all that; they never seemed to be the same girls twice.'

Angel nodded and pressed on. 'You were at the auction yesterday, weren't you? Can you tell me what you saw?'

'Oh?' Lady Ogmore shook her head, her lips tightening. 'I thought I wouldn't be able to face it. Seeing so many things I had lived with, known and handled over the years, being sold under a hammer to strangers was not something I relished. However, I was curious to see whether the sale was realizing good prices and was pleased to find it was doing quite well. I was also mildly interested to see if I knew anybody there. Indeed I spotted Sanson and I went over to him and said a brief 'hello'. But I didn't stay long.'

'Did you see anyone else, you knew?'

'Old Snatchpole, of course. That's all, I think. I had a word with the girl in the bob hole, thingie, place … just to see how things were going. Then I came out and left quickly.'

'You didn't see anything or anybody that you might have thought was suspicious?'

'No. Nothing,' she said, blowing out a length of smoke. Then she suddenly stopped. She pointed with the cigarette. 'There were two men … just behind me, I saw them at the cashier's desk … portly … with ponytails. Yes, ponytails. They looked quite incongruous at a country auction. I thought that at the time … very well turned out though. I'd take money they were in Savile Row suits.'

Angel frowned. 'Ponytails?'

4

'Come in,' the superintendent called.

Angel pushed open the door with a crutch and manoeu-vred his way into the room, reversing and turning to close the door behind him.

The superintendent looked up. 'Sit down, Michael,' he said gently. 'Take your time. Put your sticks down there.'

Angel pricked up his ears. It was unusual and worrying when Horace Harker spoke politely and called him 'Michael'. He also noticed he wasn't grinding his teeth and that he was behaving almost like a human being. Angel didn't like it at all. Something fishy was going on. He eased down into the chair, put the crutches on the floor beside him and eyed him curiously.

The superintendent reached forward, picked up an A4 sheet of paper from the pile in front of him, and went through his repertoire of face-pulling as his watery eyes skimmed the contents. 'Ah. Hmmm. Yes. Here it is. Something here, right up your street, Michael. Just come in.'

Angel nodded. It didn't sound good. He was all ears.

'You may be aware that there's a circular from London about a big, new ATM fiddle in the offing,' he began.

Angel didn't know. He shook his head.

'Yes. The banks are wetting themselves. They already lose millions a year from minor fiddles; well this is mooted to be the biggest clean-up since Catherine Zeta-Jones married Michael Douglas. It's possible they may have to shut the system down until the leak is stopped up. If one bank decides to, they all will, and that will be very embarrassing for them and damned inconvenient for the millions who depend on the hole in the wall to pay their weekly Tesco bill. They have said stand by for action. Though what they would want us to do, god knows. We couldn't covertly or openly monitor every punter at every ATM in Bromersley on *our* strength. I think the commissioner thinks we've nothing to do here but fetch cats down out of trees. Anyway, as it happens, I've got Desmond Pogle and a team running an obbo outside the new Multimass Supermarket. They've got the van with a video camera watching the ATMs. They've spotted a couple of villains working a diversion of attention scam. A new one.'

'Oh?' Angel's interest was aroused now. He liked to keep abreast of the latest tricks.

'It's quite clever,' Harker sniffed and emphasized the point by stabbing his finger in the air several times. 'As the punter enters her PIN into the ATM, the crook looks over her shoulder and records it on the keypad of his mobile phone. That looks innocent enough; he could be dialling his grandmother. Then, at the critical moment, his accomplice drops a ten-pound note on the deck behind her and says something like, 'Is this yours, love?' She turns away to look, and bends down to pick it up. The crook then leans over, takes the returned credit card out of the machine and skims it on the pocket sensor inside his jacket. It only takes a couple of seconds. She turns back to the machine, sees her cash sticking out of it and naturally reaches out for it. While she's occupied putting it safely in her purse or wherever, the crook tosses her card down to the floor by the till and leaves the scene. The accomplice points to the ground and says, 'Is that your card?' She picks it up. He then closes in on the machine, to frustrate her departure and facilitate his partner's getaway.

The punter has her card, her cash and ten pounds besides, so she'll likely toddle off delighted, blissfully unaware of what has happened. The crooks meet up later; they have her card imprint and her pin number so they're happy. They make a card up from the imprint, and they've got her pin number so they can empty her account anytime they like.'

Angel nodded. 'Very slick. You got them both?'

'No.'

Angel's eyebrows shot up. 'No?'

'We've got the accomplice. The real villain got away. He could run faster than Desmond Pogle. Hmm. He needs to take a couple of stones off, does that lad.'

Angel nodded. It was probably true.

'So now,' the superintendent said, smiling at Angel with the look of an uncle buying his favourite nephew an ice cream, 'I'm looking for a volunteer.'

Angel quickly shook his head. 'I've got a lot on, sir. With that Sanson murder.'

'And you're the one.'

The corners of Angel's mouth turned down. He didn't want lumbering with a piffling credit card fiddle and an obbo outside a supermarket. He had plenty on. He had a murder to solve. 'I haven't finished the preliminary interviews in this Sanson case yet, sir.'

The super began to grind his teeth. 'You'll soon catch up with that. You'll have to put a whip across the backs of your lads. This villain we've caught is potentially the key to much bigger fish than the killer of an out-of-work butler!'

'Oh?' Angel said thoughtfully. He didn't quite know what he meant; he certainly couldn't agree to any downgrading of the Sanson murder. 'Well sir, I can't run with crutches anyway, can I?'

'It's not about running. This lad has been processed. Pogle's interviewed him. Found virtually *nothing* out at all about him, except his name and his address in London. I should have let *you* at him. Anyway, he's been before the magistrates this morning, and was released on bail.'

34

Angel blinked. 'Released?' he said incredulously.

'Yes. But he'll be back. It'll be heard in Sheffield, in a couple of months.'

Angel shook his head. He was thinking, *they* would be lucky to see him again!

The superintendent recognized the look. 'Oh yes, Michael,' he sneered confidently. 'Oh yes. He'll be back. And do you know why I'm so positive?'

'No.'

'Because the name of this lad is Youel. Sebastian Youel,' he said with heavy emphasis. He was expecting a lively reaction from the other side of the desk.

Angel's face remained deadpan, while his mind clicked through his memory bank. There was a remarkably evil, big-time crook with that surname wanted for robbery and violence, aggravated burglary, armed bank robbery and extortion. It was an unusual name. 'Related to Harry Youel?'

The super nodded. 'His son.'

Angel looked the superintendent in the eye. 'And you have him under surveillance in the expectation of netting his father?'

The superintendent nodded with a smile bigger than Nero's on the night he murdered his own mother. 'Let's say, we're hopeful. But that's only partly correct.'

'I didn't realize he had a son.'

'Spitting image of his father.'

Angel shook his head. 'Nobody could be as ugly as Harry Youel.'

'You can see the lad for yourself in the flesh. I want you to look at Pogle's videotape. And you can get to know his face, and you can do it without him getting to know yours. You might even be able to identify his partner in crime.'

'Hmmm. And is Sebastian Youel to be kept under surveillance for the next two months?' he asked incredulously.

'It depends. But this is where you come in.' Angel knew there would be a catch.

'Well, he hasn't *seen* you. He's seen Pogle. He wouldn't know you from a stick of celery. With those crutches, you've got a perfect cover. I want you to call on the place, posing as somebody else. Confirm he's there and that he looks settled. Or not. And of course, anything else you can. You never know, his father could even be with him already! We could summon a couple of ARVs and bottle both of them, and manage without the SFO. It would be a tremendous feather in our caps, wouldn't it, Michael?'

Angel frowned. 'The SFO?'

'Aye. It's not difficult, lad. I know where he is. I know *exactly* where he is.'

Angel brightened.

The superintendent continued. 'I got Todd to follow him, and I'm in the process of organizing an FSG from Wakefield to take over full-time surveillance if needs be. We haven't the manpower and, in any case, the Chief doesn't want us to throw money about on this long shot. We've had a very expensive year and the thought of mounting an operation of this sort would bring back his shingles!'

Angel rubbed his chin. 'You are expecting Sebastian to lead you to his father?'

'Inevitable, I would have thought,' the super replied with a grin.

Angel nodded. He could be right. 'Where is the lad now then, sir?'

'Oh, not far away. Two hours ago, he was traced to that little posh private kindergarten, Littlecombe, on the Huddersfield Road. Young Todd is in an unmarked car on his own, on the road, monitoring him. But what that villain's doing at a nippers' school, I can't imagine.'

*

Angel returned to his office and slammed the door. He snatched up the phone and tapped in a number. There was a click and a voice answered: 'Yes sir?'

'Something's cropped up, Ron.' He sniffed. 'I want you back here, smartish.'

'Right, sir,' Gawber said.

'How's that listing going?'

'All right. Mr Snatchpole's here, helping me out. Trevor Crisp and Ed Scrivens are both out on the knocker.'

'Leave them to it. Put your foot down. I'll be in the viewing room.'

'Right sir.'

Gawber was back at the station in eight minutes, and joined Angel who was viewing the videotape of the ATM scam.

The clarity and colour of the pictures was good. Young Youel was a short, well-dressed man in a dark tweed suit and light blue open-necked shirt. His hair was combed down tidily on a head the shape of a football. He rarely opened his eyes fully; the half-closed eyelids sometimes gave him an oriental look. He never smiled, but like the photographs of his father, he had a mouthful of big teeth. Youel's partner in crime was unremarkable in his appearance: in his twenties, fair-haired, spotty, with scruffy jeans, T-shirt, baseball cap and trainers. Neither of the two policemen knew either man. Angel reckoned they had probably come into the manor from away.

They moved to Angel's office and listened to the tape of the interview Pogle had conducted with Youel. The young villain spoke slowly and pronounced every syllable distinctly. He had said he was twenty years of age, although he looked older, and gave an address in south London as his place of residence. He denied the charge of 'conspiracy to fraud' and pleaded not guilty.

Angel phoned the council offices in Croydon and charmingly persuaded a clerk there to consult the electoral roll. The young man duly reported back that a Sebastian Youel had lived in a flat there for the last twelve months and was registered as its sole occupant.

Angel and Gawber then left the station together for Littlecombe. Gawber was behind the wheel and turned left out of the street and on to Huddersfield Road. They went round the roundabout that sported the fountain known as 'Victoria Falls' with its powerful spray of water and colourful show of spring flowers. They shot passed the Ogmore Hall gates and up the hill. Soon they were in the country whizzing past budding hawthorn bushes and bluebells waving at them from each side of the road.

Angel could only wonder what the villain was doing at this infants' school in the Yorkshire countryside. There weren't any rich pickings there.

He sniffed and turned to Gawber. 'I went to that school briefly, you know, as a pupil.'

'Oh yes?' Gawber said as he pressed his foot hard on the accelerator to overtake a tractor towing a trailer of artichokes.

'Aye. In the days when my mother thought she would try and make a gentleman out of me … have me learn elocution and botany, and how to play the violin. And avoid getting impetigo and nits from the kids at the wood school. Yes. Learn to say 'please' and 'thank you'. Not drop my aitches … mix with a better class of infant.'

'Did it do you any good, sir?'

He paused, rubbed his chin and then shook his head. 'Still got nits.'

Gawber smiled.

'There'll be no kids there, today, sir. It's the Easter holidays.'

'Aye. Aye. Hmmm. That's right,' he said, nodding thoughtfully. He spotted a car with a familiar licence plate parked on a patch of grass at the side of the road. He pointed at it through the windscreen. 'That'll be Todd.'

Gawber slowed down and pulled up alongside the detective constable's car. Angel lowered the window.

Todd spotted him and leaned out of the car window.

'Now lad,' Angel said. 'What's happening?'

'He's still in there, sir,' Todd said indicating the road ahead with his thumb.

'Did you actually see him arrive and go into the school?'

'Yes sir. He came from town by taxi. I saw him pay the taxi off and walk straight in through the front door.'

'He didn't knock?'

'No, sir. Just walked straight in.'

'Right,' Angel said frowning. 'And he didn't see you?'

'No sir,' the young man said confidently. 'I dodged behind a tree.'

Angel hoped he was right. 'Right, lad.' He nodded to Gawber to drive on. Two hundred yards further along the road, they reached a large stone-built house surrounded by tall, leafy trees, a high wall and open iron gates supported by two stone pillars. Gawber slowed down at the entrance where there was a neat wooden signboard, painted white on green. It read: 'St Veronica's School, for Boys and Girls between the ages of six and ten. Headteacher and proprietor: Cynthia C. Fiske MA, BA, Oxon.'

Gawber drove through the gates, round to his right by a neat lawn bordered by wallflowers and then pulled on the brake by the front steps.

Angel opened the door. 'Wait here for me.'

Gawber switched off the engine and passed him the crutches. Angel took them. He sensed Gawber was apprehensive so he nodded reassuringly. He made his way across the drive and struggled up the three steps to a stone-flagged area covered by a green-timbered canopy overhanging the front door. He pressed the shiny brass button and heard the bell ring inside. He took a step backwards and waited … and waited. There was no reply. He pursed his lips and kept repositioning his fingers round the grips on the crutches. Meanwhile he looked down over his shoulder at Gawber who was peering up at him. Angel turned back to the door, leaned forward and was about to press the bell push again when he heard a few rapid footsteps. The big door opened ten inches, and a head appeared in the gap. It was unmistakably Harry Youel's son, Sebastian. The round head and the big teeth were not a pretty sight.

Angel's pulse raced and his chest burned inexplicably.

The young man's expressionless face looked out at him. No smile. Eyes half closed. 'What can I do for you?' he said in a dreamy, continental voice.

'Good afternoon. My name is Angel, Michael Angel. I would like to speak to Miss Cynthia Fiske?' he asked looking confident. He hadn't the slightest idea of what he was going to say to her.

The door was suddenly pulled open more widely by an unseen hand to reveal a dark-haired, tall woman aged about forty-five. She was neat and smart, in a plain, dark dress and black low-heeled shoes. She had not a hair out of place and had that freshly scrubbed appearance of a no-nonsense, no-frills, professional woman.

She looked enquiringly down at him. 'I'm Cynthia Fiske. Good afternoon. What can I do for you?' she said with a practised smile.

Sebastian stared at her briefly. He wasn't pleased. He said nothing but quickly turned away and charged up the staircase opposite the door, two steps at a time.

Angel pursed his lips. He wasn't certain what he wanted to say next. The aim was to get into the house. He wanted to see what was happening.

'I wonder if I could see you about my son?' he said, surprised at his spontaneous creativeness.

She hesitated for a moment, then glancing at his crutches, she stepped to one side and said, 'Of course, Mr Angel. Please come in.'

'Thank you,' Angel said with a smile. She seemed wholly taken in by the deception. It was looking good. He swung the crutches on to the wooden floor. The hall was much smaller than he remembered it, but the dark oak panelling, paintwork and stained floorboards seemed to be exactly the same.

'Do please follow me,' she said after closing the door. She led the way across the hall, past the bottom of the wide staircase and the doors to the basement and schoolroom, into a comfortable room with a French window. He remembered that it used to be the headmistress's study but now it seemed to serve as a multi-purpose reception room.

She held the door open for him and closed it when he had swung the crutches inside.

'Please sit down,' she said gliding across to a chair by a small desk against the wall.

'It's a lovely house you have here,' Angel remarked as he eased into an armchair opposite her.

'I like it,' she said smiling easily, but he thought it might not have been the genuine article.

He carefully lowered the crutches to the floor. 'I thought it would be a good time to come, when all the children are on holiday, and the school is closed,' he said, hoping it might prompt her to explain the presence of young Youel.

She didn't take the bait. She simply nodded.

'I believe you wanted to tell me about your son.'

'Yes,' he went on, wondering what to say next.

'Were you thinking of sending him here?'

Angel nodded. 'He's very introverted. I would like him to come out of himself. And, of course, I want him to be well educated.'

'Do you mean he's shy? Have you not brought him with you?'

'No.'

'That's a pity. I would need to see him before I could make any recommendations. I have vacancies for two pupils at the moment, but I have a couple with a 7-year-old girl coming to see me again tomorrow. She is a delightful child and I dare say she will fill one of the vacancies; then I shall have just one open position next term, which incidentally starts in a fortnight. I tell you what, Mr Angel. I will give you my brochure listing all the special subject classes, school uniform requirements, dates and times, tariff and terms. You and your wife — you have a wife, Mr Angel?'

'Oh yes.'

'You and your wife can study it, and perhaps give me a ring.'

She opened a bureau drawer, took out a cream booklet and passed it over to him. He glanced at the cover, then put the brochure in his pocket.

She crossed to the door. 'You can give me a ring in a day or so,' she said. 'And bring your son to see me, if you wish, and we'll see what we can do. I will wait to hear from you.'

The interview was over. She clearly wasn't going to offer to show him round the school; it would have been unsubtle of him to have suggested it. There was nothing more he could do. He thanked her politely and reached down for the crutches. She led the way across the hall and opened the front door. They exchanged smiles, then he turned and picked his way down the three steps while he heard the heavy door close behind him. He crossed the drive to the car and reached out for the door handle. As it opened, Gawber anxiously leaned across and said, 'I've just had the super on the phone. There's been another stabbing.'

His eyebrows shot up. 'What?' he said, handing Gawber the crutches.

'A woman called Alison Drabble. She lives in the town. The super's sent SOC, two uniformed and Dr Mac. I've got the address,' he said and started the engine.

Angel lowered himself into the seat and closed the car door. 'Aye. Right.' Their car sped through the gates up to the main road. 'Alison Drabble?' Angel muttered.

'Yes. Do you know her?'

'No,' he frowned. 'But the name's familiar. Drabble … Drabble.'

Gawber pressed the car hurriedly on to the main road back to Bromersley.

Angel's eyes suddenly opened wide. 'I remember. Yes. I do remember. That was the name of the housekeeper to the Ogmores. She knew Sanson, the butler. They'd worked together for years. Hmmm. I needed to speak to her about him.' He looked out of the window and sniffed. 'Can't ask her much now, can I?' he said irritably.

Gawber made good speed down the long hill past Ogmore Hall, then slowed to go round Victoria Falls roundabout and then changed gear to go up the hill into Bromersley. They soon reached town, and he drove rapidly through it to the big new Sanderson estate on the west side.

'That flat is in a block on the left, I think, sir. Number twenty-four.'

Angel spotted a white transit van, a police car and an unmarked car parked close together on the grass verge two hundred yards ahead. 'They're there, look.'

Gawber pulled up next to Dr Mac's car. Three women with bare, fat arms were leaning over their respective front gates of neighbouring houses. As Angel and Gawber got out of the car, they stared at them in silence, and watched them enter the building.

Number twenty-four was on the ground floor along a tiled corridor. Four of the six doors the policemen had to pass were wide open, and women — some of them with small children — stood there in silence, watching the comings and goings.

A uniformed constable was outside the open door of number twenty-four. He saw Angel and Gawber approach. 'Good afternoon, sir.'

'Afternoon, sarge.'

Angel nodded in response and leaned on his crutches out in the corridor; he peered through the door. He could see Dr Mac in his white paper overalls bending over something on the bed. 'Is it all right to come in, Mac?'

'Oh. That you Mike? Hang on a minute, will you?' he called. 'Just getting the body away.'

Two men in green overalls, hats and masks rushed up behind Angel carrying a stretcher and a sheet. The inspector stepped back. They pushed in front of him up to the open door.

The PC said, 'Hold on, lads. This is still a crime scene.' He pushed his nose through the doorway and called in. 'Hey Doc. They're here from the mortuary. Can they come in?'

'Aye. Come on in lads,' Mac called out. 'Mind where you tread.'

They went in. Nobody spoke. Mac pointed to the bed. On it was the body of a middle-aged woman; she was on her back with her arms outstretched, wearing a blouse, skirt, stockings and a slipper on her left foot. The other slipper was on the floor at the side of the bed. Her head was turned facing the window. The top half of her was saturated in blood, as was the bed. Her face, arms and hands were white, wrinkle-free and shiny. Although her eyes were closed, her mouth was open showing a displaced upper denture sited grotesquely askew. Her hair was neat and crimped, like a wig.

The two men didn't waste any time. They covered the body in the white sheet and transferred it to the stretcher. As they made for the door, Mac noticed red stains seeping through the sheet. 'Get it away quickly, lads. There are a lot of ghouls out there.'

'Yes doc.'

The men manoeuvred the stretcher through the doorway and then walked at a brisk pace down the corridor, passing the women standing in the open doorways.

Angel heard a few wails. He wasn't surprised and just shook his head. Gawber and Angel looked away from each other.

Mac stuck his nose out of the door. 'Come in, Mike. There isn't much room.'

A SOCO carrying a camera came out of the door at the other side of the fireplace and signalled to Dr Mac who went out with him.

Angel swung the crutches inside the doorway. The carpet was covered with a white sheet, which showed small areas of fresh blood oozing through here and there. Gawber stepped in beside him. They stood in awe as they looked round the tiny bed-sitting room. The few pictures and photographs in frames on the walls were all askew. The floor was covered with books, newspapers, clothes, coathangers and bottles of tablets. Ornaments had been indiscriminately turned out of the bookcase, the bedside cabinet, the wall cupboard and the wardrobe and unceremoniously strewn on the floor like worthless litter. The blankets and sheets on the bed had been removed to reveal the mattress, on to which the victim, bleeding profusely, had collapsed. The doctor came back into the room. Angel said, 'How many rooms are there, Mac?'

'There's a bathroom, toilet and dining kitchen, that's all.'

'Are they all like this?'

'Yes,' Mac said, his jaw set tight. He looked round the room. 'It's been done thoroughly.'

'Aye, but not by a professional.' He pointed to a tallboy whose six drawers had been pulled out completely, the contents tipped on to the floor, and then slung upturned against the wall.

'Wouldn't you say it was the same MO as the Geoffrey Sanson murder, sir?'

'Aye. Looks like it. And there'd not be much money here … and she's not likely to be in the drug racket, either using or dealing,' Angel said. He turned to the doctor. 'What you found, Mac?'

'There's no forensic. The murderer was wearing leather or rubber gloves, so no prints. It's bone dry outside, so there's no footmarks. No body liquids from the intruder, so no DNA.'

Angel grunted. 'It's going to be one of those cases.'

Mac continued: 'The woman was stabbed … between the ribs into the heart, the same as Sanson. Died instantly. And like Sanson, it was a stiletto, and it was stuck in with the precision of a butcher's hand and left there.'

He wrinkled his nose. 'The murderer would be blooded?'

'Oh yes. On the hand and wrist at the very minimum … probably the arm and chest as well. Get me the murderer's clothes now and I'll get you a guilty verdict.'

Angel sniffed. 'How long has she been dead?'

'Maybe twelve or eighteen hours.'

'Anybody else live here … with her? Any signs of a partner? Husband, boyfriend, girlfriend, mother, daughter?'

'Looks like she lived on her own.'

'Any other wounds?'

'Don't know.'

'Sanson had bruises to his stomach, didn't he?'

'Aye. Several. Probably caused by a clenched fist.'

He turned back to Gawber. 'Have a look and see if that door's been forced.'

Gawber got down on one knee. He called up to the doctor. 'Has this door been printed, sir?'

'Aye. Wiped clean … or gloves.'

'Who found her?' Angel asked.

'Next-door neighbour,' Mac said.

Gawber stood up. 'It's not been forced, sir. Key's in the lock on the inside. She let her murderer in.'

Angel pulled a face. 'Why do they always do that?' he said grimly. He looked down the corridor and said, 'Ask around. See what you can find out.'

Gawber nodded and went out.

Angel turned to Mac. 'What do you think then, Mac? Off the top of your head? Money, drugs, booze, sex, rape … jealous ex-husband … row with boyfriend … what do you reckon? What's your instinct?'

Dr Mac peeled off the plastic gloves and pulled back the white hood. 'Robbery, I'd say. What else? Respectable middle-aged woman, lives on her own, easy target.'

'*Apparently* respectable.'

'Ah, well,' he shrugged. 'She *knew* her killer.'

'Mmmm. She was apparently willing to let him in. No sign of a struggle. Not a hair out of place. Cold-blooded job. Didn't rough her up. Looks like he gained admittance easily, probably simply knocked on the door. 'Come to read the meter, love.' 'I'm from the town hall. It's about a rates rebate.' 'I'm from the lottery: you've won a million pounds!' Any old tale.'

'Doesn't have to be a man. It could have been a woman.'

'Yeah. Yeah,' Angel said rubbing his chin. 'Their homes taken to pieces in the same way … and they both got stuck with a knife in the chest, on the same day … and both had worked for the Ogmores?'

'Sounds like somebody under a great deal of pressure,' Mac said wiping his hands on a clean piece of cotton wool.

'Aye,' Angel said, still rubbing his chin.

5

There was a knock on the door.

'Come in.'

It was Gawber.

'Good morning, sir.'

'Is it?' He sniffed. 'Aye, well, sit down, lad. What have you got?'

'The woman next door found Alison Drabble's body. She wanted to return a magazine she had borrowed from her. She said that she knocked on the door about two-thirty and got no reply. It was unusual at that time. She went away and came back half an hour later, knocked again and this time tried the door. It wasn't locked, so she peeped inside and called out. She saw her on the bed, covered in blood. She didn't go in. She closed the door, went back to her own flat, had a sip of brandy then dialled triple nine.'

Angel nodded. 'It was reported at 1545. Anybody see anything?'

'Not exactly,' Gawber said, hesitantly, then he added, 'There was a blind man passing the front of the flats at about two o'clock.'

Angel's eyes lit up. 'That could be about the right time!' Then he frowned. 'A blind man! A blind witness isn't much good?'

'Now there's a funny thing, sir,' Gawber said. 'The man said he walks with his guide dog past the flats about that time most days. He was coming back from having his dinner with his sister-in-law on the other side of the estate. He walked through the recreation ground and said he was nearly run down by a high-powered car at the gate. That's only fifty yards from the flat.'

'So what?'

'Well, it's the place the murderer probably parked his car.'

'Aye,' Angel said tetchily. 'But a blind man?'

'Well, this man, Neville Mountjoy, he's in his fifties, he reckons he could recognize the sound of the car if he was to hear it again.'

Angel pursed his lips, then shook his head. 'Can't imagine what a jury might think of a blind witness who identifies cars by the sound of their engines. It's very clever, but it sounds like a novelty act from one of those daft Saturday night TV shows.'

'Not only the car engine. He can identify the differences in the sound of brakes, gear changes, reversing and so on. He used to be a car mechanic, before he went blind.'

'Hmmm. Poor chap. It's not a wealthy neighbourhood for a powerful car to frequent, is it? He's positive the driver nearly hit him?'

'Well, yes.'

Angel rubbed his chin. 'So the driver ... the murderer would remember the incident, wouldn't he? That could be *very* important.'

'I should think so. The car braked hard, reversed and then moved off again. It was hearing the different sounds made by the car so close to him that make him confident he would be able to identify it if it came anywhere near him again.'

49

Angel frowned and shook his head. 'Still, I can't see the CPS putting a blind man in the box as a witness ... because he claims he can positively identify a car by the sounds it makes.'

'Perhaps not, but it might help the investigation.'

Angel nodded. 'It might, lad. It might. You are right. I must see the man urgently. See what he has to say. Let me have his address. Anything else? Did you manage to unearth any muck or scandal about her?'

Gawber's eyebrows shot up. 'No. She seemed a perfectly respectable woman. Neighbours all seemed to like her, sir. Not a bad word to say about her. She hasn't been there long, about four months, but she seemed popular enough.'

'What did she do for a living?'

'She wasn't in employment. She had been looking for a job since she stopped working for Lady Ogmore and had to move out of the cottage.'

'Mmm.' Angel wrinkled his nose and looked down thoughtfully. He was quiet for a moment. Then, suddenly, he looked up. His face had changed. His jaw dropped. His eyes were shining. 'Hey, I've just realized. Seeing as these two victims both worked at Ogmore Hall, I wonder if the others who worked there might be in danger too!'

Gawber's jaw dropped.

Angel stabbed into his pocket and pulled out the card Lady Ogmore had given him the previous day. He read off the phone number and then dialled it. The ringing tone began. It continued ... and continued ... but there was no reply.

*

The car came to a stop with a screech of brakes outside the bungalow. Angel threw open the door and heaved himself out. Gawber passed him the crutches and the big man swiftly manoeuvred himself up to the garden gate. It was unfastened and swinging ominously in the breeze. He didn't like the

50

look of it. He rocked the crutches straight up the short path to the front door. He tried the door but it was locked. He glanced round at the windows on the front elevation; they were all intact.

Gawber overtook him and ran round to the rear of the building.

Angel picked up the door knocker and banged it hard on the door six times. There was no response. He banged again and yelled, 'This is the police. Open up. This is the police!'

There was still no reply.

Angel tried again. 'This is the police. Open up.'

Seconds later Gawber came round the corner of the bungalow and up to the inspector. His face told the story. 'There *has* been a break-in, sir. A window has been smashed. I'm going in!'

'No you're not! He might still be in there,' Angel called. 'You stay here. Watch the front, and phone in. I'll take a look.' He pointed the crutches determinedly along the flagged path.

The sergeant looked anxiously after him as he tapped into his mobile.

Angel arrived at the rear of the bungalow. He soon found the smashed window. A double-glazed pane had been efficiently knocked out, leaving a hole big enough for a man to climb through. He looked at the fragments of glass spread over the path, the adjacent border of expired daffodils and thriving dandelions, and the lawn. He then peered through the jagged glass at the thick burgundy curtains inside, which were closed and quivering slightly with the breeze. He raised one of his crutches and poked into the curtains looking for a gap. When he found one, he pursed his lips, sucked in a long steady breath of air and eased the curtain to one side. His pulse quickened as he looked into the room. He wasn't surprised at what he saw. Nearest the window was a double bed with the blankets, covers and sheets stripped off, revealing the ticking; spread across it was a mishmash of pieces of shiny pink and white underwear, curious pieces of delicate lace lingerie with narrow straps, a jumble of black and brown stockings, twenty or more pink hair rollers, a bottle of a brown liquid with 'Chanel' on the label, four different pots of cream, a packet of paracetamol tablets, a pair of pliers and several handwritten envelopes. Beyond, by the door, seven empty dressing-table drawers were piled up in a heap next to an upturned linen basket. Next to that was a cream and gold wardrobe, the door was open and swinging free; it squeaked like a cantankerous cat as the draught from the window changed its position from time to time. At the far side of the room, a 'Do Not Disturb' sign, probably lifted from some exotic hotel in the past, was hanging irrelevantly from the knob of the door which led into the hall, where he could just see an upturned dressing-table stool, its feet pointing heavenward.

There was no sign of life … or death.

Everything was quiet and still. Only the wind and the rustle of the rose bushes and the cypresses that bordered the little back garden behind him disturbed the silence. He lowered the crutch letting the curtain drop back into place.

He sighed.

The rest of the bungalow needed searching and it needed doing quickly. He tried not to think about what might be waiting for him in one of the other rooms.

The sudden roar of a car engine, then brakes, then car doors slamming caught his attention. He turned, stabbed the crutches on to the flags and sped up to the front of the bungalow.

At the gate was a police car with a blue light flashing. Two men in helmets and body armour armed with Glock 17s were running up the path.

Angel's face brightened.

Gawber looked at the men and blew out a long breath.

'There's a window broken at the back.' Angel called. 'Go careful. There might be a welcoming committee with a knife inside waiting for you.'

'Right, sir.' They dashed off.

'When you get in there, open this door,' he called after them.

A white van drove up and parked next to the two cars. In it were two men from the SOC team. Angel noticed them, but he was keeping his eye on the front door. They got out of the van and yelled over the fence.

'Good morning, sir.'

'My word. You're early birds,' he quipped. 'Who's sent you?'

'The super, sir,' one of them replied.

Angel nodded. 'Mmm. Aren't you getting enough work?'

They were always being chided. SOCOs were regarded as being on a cushy number. They weren't closely supervised and were thought to make their jobs last as long as they liked. The sergeant ignored the jibe. 'What you got, sir?'

Angel continued watching the door. 'A housebreaking, at the moment. I'll tell you more when I know it.'

The men returned to the van, opened the door and pulled out a big sealed polythene bag with new paper overalls in it.

Angel heard some movement from inside the bungalow. 'Ah!' he said and moved up to the door. He heard a key turn in the lock, a chain rattled and the door opened. The two armed policemen appeared.

Angel moved up to them. 'Well?' he said anxiously.

'All clear downstairs, sir. But it's a mess. Phew! It's been well and truly turned over.'

'But there's nobody in there?'

'No, sir. We have checked the loft and there isn't a cellar. We haven't checked it for explosives.'

Angel blew out a long length of warm air. 'That's all right, lads. Thank you. Stand down now and report back to the station.'

They made their way down the path to their car.

Angel moved up to the door. The loud roar of a vehicle arriving caught his attention. He looked back. It was an open-topped white Porsche sports car. In the driving-seat was Lady Ogmore in a tight-fitting powder-blue trouser suit. She pulled up outside the gate, her eyes staring, her mouth open. She slowly got out of the car, taking in the policemen and the vehicles. She closed the car door and toddled unsteadily in her Gucci shoes up the path to Angel and, flashing her eyes, said, 'Whatever is happening, inspector?'

*

'What!' the super bellowed, waving his arms over the desk. 'It's damned lucky she *was* out. If she had been in his way, he would have most certainly murdered her!'

Angel sighed. 'She had been down town shopping, sir. She'd been gone about two hours. The burglar alarm didn't go off because she didn't set it. She is a bit slap happy. She left the front door key in the lock on the inside!'

He stopped grinding his teeth. 'And nothing was taken?'

'No. And the place was dripping with valuables you could easily slip into your pocket.'

'That's a funny thing. Hmm. Any forensic?'

'No. No fingerprints, DNA or footprints; Mac doesn't hold out any hope.'

'Have you done the house-to-house?'

'There aren't any neighbours out there, sir. Nearest neighbour would be about half a mile.'

'Hmmm. Well, wrap it up quickly then. You satisfied it is the same party that has stabbed that butler chap, Sanson, and that woman, Alison Drabble?'

'All three houses ransacked in the same amateurish way, and all linked with Ogmore Hall.'

'I don't like this. I don't like this at all. This is very nasty! It's like the plague. It's two bodies in two days. And the villain's not taken anything. He's looking, but not finding. If he found what he wanted, he'd stop. What do you reckon he's after?'

'Something small. If it was something big, he wouldn't have to search so thoroughly.'

'Aye,' he sniffed. 'But what is it that's worth two lives?'

Angel said, 'Don't know. I'm worried about a young woman who was Lord Ogmore's secretary, sir. Kate Cumberland. Can't trace her. Lady Ogmore doesn't know where she went to. She left about a year ago, just after he died. She could be next.'

*

'Come in,' Angel called angrily.

It was Ahmed. 'You looking for me, sir?'

'There you are,' he bawled. 'Where have you been hiding? You're harder to find than Houdini's rabbit.'

Ahmed's eyes opened wide.

'I've only been in the CID office, sir,' he protested.

'Aye, well, I've got a little job for you. I want you to find a misper.'

Ahmed frowned. 'A misper?'

'A missing person,' he growled impatiently. 'We've no idea where she is. We don't think she has a record. It's necessary for her safety to find her to protect her from this killer. Her name is Kate Cumberland. She's aged about thirty-five. Worked at Ogmore Hall until a year ago. We've got to find her quickly. Now start with the electoral roll. She was living at the Hall a year ago. Now she has moved on. Well, get on with it, lad. It's a matter of life and death!'

'Right sir,' Ahmed said and dashed out of the office.

Angel leaned back in the swivel chair. He wished there was a quick way to find this woman; the trouble was the people who might have known her whereabouts were now dead.

There was a knock at the door.

'Come in.'

It was Dr Mac.

'Ah!' Angel's eyes lit up. 'Come in, Mac. Come in. Sit down,' he said, pushing the papers in front of him to the far side of the desk. He was hopeful that the doctor might throw some new light on the case. 'What do you know?'

Mac was carrying a big manilla envelope. 'I've got something to show you.' He opened the envelope and pulled out two clear-plastic self-seal bags and placed them on the desk in front of him.

Angel could see that each bag contained a stiletto, designed like a miniature sword. He reached forward, opened one of the bags and carefully took out the knife. The blade was 8" long and the handle 4". The three-sided steel blade was honed down at the tip almost to the sharpness of a needle. On both sides of the silver handle was an engraving of a long sword with a snake twined around it, and on the pommel was the head of a lion.

Angel turned it round in his hand and pulled a face. 'The murderer would need to carry it around in a scabbard or holster or something, so that it didn't stick into him or his clothing or anything else?'

'Almost certainly. Leather I suppose. Strapped to the arm.'

'Or the chest. Yeah.'

Mac said, 'These were made in Italy, about 1900. They are copies of originals dated about the middle of the seventeenth century. Steel blade, silver handle. The originals are much sought after for their antique value and interest.'

'Are these two the same?'

'Identical. Probably from a set of six.'

Angel pulled a face. 'Hmm. I hope we don't see the other four!'

Mac looked at him. 'Have you any idea who you are looking for?'

'Not yet,' he sniffed. 'You've given us nothing up to now.'

Mac shook his head. 'You need a profiler.'

'I've got one.'

'Who?'

'Me.'

Mac smiled wryly.

Angel said, 'I went on a course last year. I was second from the top at Hendon.'

'I beg your pardon,' Mac said with an apologetic smile.

'I know exactly the sort of person we are looking for. We want someone who has a fixation on one particular goal, and whatever it is, nothing and nobody will stop him or her from reaching it. They won't be put off by anything. Cannot be moved away from the target. And not interested in small rewards … just the big prize!'

'Anything else?'

'Yes. They are not right in the head. There'll be some quirk in their personality that will give them away. You watch.'

'I hope you're right.'

'So do I. Before anybody else gets skewered.'

Mac looked at him with narrowed eyes. 'Haven't you anything at all?'

'Yep. Got an eye witness.'

Mac beamed. 'That's great.'

'Huh,' Angel said, shaking his head.

Mac frowned. 'What's the matter?'

'He's blind.'

*

Angel picked up the phone and dialled a number. It rang out for a few moments then there was a click. He bawled into the mouthpiece: 'Hello! Is that Lord Lucan?'

'No sir. It's DS Crisp.'

'I thought you were dead,' he growled. 'You've been away that long.'

'Still very busy with this inquiry, sir. I'm on Charles Street,' he said smartly.

'Haven't heard a word from you. Are Ron Gawber and young Scrivens there?'

'Ed Scrivens is on a call round the corner. Don't know where Ron is, sir. He's working off his own list.'

'Hmmm. Well, what have *you* got, lad? Found anybody who saw anything?'

'Lots of witnesses. But they didn't see anything.'

'What about the people standing *next* to him, at the back of the room?'

'Nobody *admits* to standing next to him, sir. Since the news of Mrs Drabble's murder, some of the punters are nervous at even being interviewed.'

Angel was well aware of the situation. The national newspapers had got hold of the story and reports with photographs of the front of Snatchpole's auction house, the block of flats where Mrs Drabble's body was found, and an old, fuzzy picture of Geoffrey Sanson dug up from somewhere, had appeared in all the tabloids. The general public were avidly soaking up the news, but with the motive for the murders unknown, the locals could not be certain they were not to be the next potential victim. The murderer was clearly someone among them.

'Have you seen a Dr Sinclair yet?'

'No sir. We know about him. He's on my list. I'll get round to him.'

'Let *me* interview him. He lives up Creeford Avenue, not far from you. Call in and explain I'm temporarily on crutches, and ask him if he'd be kind enough to call in at the station. Urgently.'

'Right, sir.'

6

'This won't take long, doctor,' Angel said. 'You were at the auction on Monday and attended Geoffrey Sanson just before he died?'

'Yes. He wasn't one of my patients. I'm retired, you know. But yes, I did. Poor man. The dagger went right into the heart, through the aorta — terrible. I couldn't do anything for him.'

'Did he say anything before he died?'

'No. He would have lost consciousness instantly. He said nothing.'

'Whereabouts were you in the saleroom, in relation to him?'

'At the front. On the front row.'

'And whereabouts was Mr Sanson?'

'He was directly behind me, but right at the back. I believe he was standing against the wall.'

Angel nodded. 'What exactly happened?'

'Well, I suppose the sale was about halfway through, and Snatchpole was going into raptures about an oil painting on the wall on the right. My attention was on the painting. Suddenly, there was a bit of a commotion behind me. I heard several gasps ... a woman screamed. I looked round.

Someone said a man had fainted ... someone else said he was bleeding. Lots of people stood up. Snatchpole called from the podium and asked me if I would take a look. I made my way to the back of the hall. A man was collapsed on the floor; there was a crowd of people round him. He was already covered in blood. There was no pulse. I told Snatchpole he was dead and to send for the police. People were pushing and gawping and asking questions. My wife was upset. We left immediately, and went straight home.'

'Did you know the man?'

'I didn't *know* him, but I knew who he was. He was always there when I called on the Ogmores. Pleasant enough chap. He was present in the room when Archie died, last year.'

'You were the Ogmores' doctor?'

'And Archie's father and mother before him ... and, although I am retired, I still look after Lady Emerald.'

'You didn't see anything suspicious or unusual ... anyone behaving strangely?'

'No, well, we were anxious to leave.'

'Hmmm. Sanson had some bruising on his stomach wall. The pathologist says it was probably caused by him being punched several times with clenched fists. Did you see anything that would support that theory?'

'No. But I didn't examine him, inspector.'

'No. No. Hmmm. Did you see anybody at the auction that you knew?'

'Oh yes. I was seated quite near to Mrs Buller-Price, and I saw Lady Emerald briefly, at a distance ... I knew Snatchpole, of course. I don't think I remember anybody else.'

'You didn't see two men in their fifties with ponytails, did you?'

The doctor smiled. 'No.'

Angel stood up. 'Thanks very much, doctor. I told you it wouldn't take long.'

'I hope you get the murderer very soon.'

Angel nodded firmly. 'We will. You can be sure of that.'

The two men shook hands.

Ahmed escorted the doctor up to reception and then came back to the inspector's office. Angel was looking out of the window and rubbing his chin.

'Now lad,' he said, looking round. 'Have you found that missing woman, Kate Cumberland, yet?'

'No sir.'

'Well, you'd better get straight back to that then. Every second's delay puts that woman's life at risk.'

*

Angel picked up the phone and tapped in a number.

'Traffic.'

'Michael Angel here. I need a lift home.'

'Nothing in at the moment, inspector. Can do ... in about five or ten minutes. At the front.'

'Thank you,' Angel said and replaced the phone. He was glad to be going home. He grabbed his coat from the hook and made for the door. He swung the crutches rhythmically up the green corridor to the security door, tapped in the code and made his way through it, across the reception area and out through the glass door into the fresh air. He stood on the top step and looked down. At the bottom, against the kerb, parked on the wrong side was a little red car. It was the only vehicle there. He made his way down the steps. When he was at the bottom, the driver leaned out of the window and said, 'Inspector Angel?'

'Yes, lad,' he replied.

The young man in the car nodded and threw open the passenger door from the inside.

'Thanks. I want to go to the Forest Hill estate.'

'Right, sir.'

Angel put the crutches on the back seat and eased himself down into the little car and closed the door. He put on the seat belt.

The driver let in the clutch sharply and they pulled away from the kerb with an unexpected shudder and a squeal of the tyres.

Angel looked at the young fresh face. 'I don't recognize you, lad. You must be new. What's your name?'

'Smith, sir.'

Angel rubbed his chin.

Smith then made a jerky U-turn, went to the end of Church Street and turned left into Market Street.

Angel lowered his eyebrows. 'Take it easy now. There's no rush. We don't need to go through town.'

'It'll be all right, sir,' Smith said pressing on the accelerator.

Angel's mouth tightened. 'It would be better to go by the ring road.'

'Do you think so?' the young man said, swiftly pulling into a long stream of traffic heading for Edensor Street, the shopping centre.

Angel shook his head impatiently. 'It's too late now. You can't turn back. You'll have to go through the town, and there are *four* sets of traffic lights. And all the traffic for Sheffield and Barnsley trying to get away.'

There were cars and buses in front, behind and at the side of them. They slowed to a snail's pace. The car came to a halt behind a red bus.

Women with bags and parcels appeared from all directions and began to leap up the step into the bus.

Angel patiently watched the tedious loading process in front of them. He sighed loudly.

'It won't take long, sir. We'll soon have you there.'

Angel groaned silently. He hated being pacified. 'Where are you from, lad? You don't live round here?'

'No sir.'

A cloud of black fumes blew out from the back of the bus as it moved off. Smith let in the clutch and said, 'We're away again, sir.'

'Aye,' Angel growled.

The car slowly picked up speed.

Suddenly, out of his eye corner, Angel saw a figure step off the pavement on the nearside on to the road in front of the bus. The bus driver braked. Smith braked. There was a jerk followed by a thud and an expensive, crunchy, splintering noise from behind.

Angel groaned.

Smith pulled a face and said, 'Oh.' He pulled on the brake, unfastened his seat belt   and got out of the car.

Angel rubbed his chin hard and looked round to see if he could catch sight of the driver of the vehicle behind. All he could see was a street full of traffic, now stationary in both directions, and crowded by pedestrians with shopping. He pulled a face and wondered what time he would get home that night.

The bus pulled away again, leaving the road ahead clear. He was stranded in the car on a busy road in the centre of town with the engine running and no driver. He rubbed his chin again and looked round. It was then he noticed there was no radio kit fitted below the dash. This wasn't a station car; must be the driver's own car. He felt a bit guilty complaining.

The car door was suddenly snatched open and a man jumped in. He was big. He was wearing a dark suit, white shirt and navy blue tie. A gold earring glinted in his thick earlobe. The smell of Taiwan brandy drifted under Angel's nostrils.

He glared at the big man and reached out with both hands for the man's arm and locked on to it in a grip of steel. 'What you doing, lad? What's your game?'

'Mr Angel?' the intruder said with a smile like a Bechstein keyboard.

'Mebbe,' he said, working on the principle that he never gave information away for nothing. 'Who are you?' he snarled.

The doors behind him opened; two more men climbed into the car. His eyebrows shot up.

The doors slammed shut.

Something was wrong. He licked his lips. Something was *very* wrong. His heart began to race. He didn't like the odds. He turned to look.

Strong, sweaty hands grabbed his head at the temples and forced it back to the front.

'Don't be difficult, Mr Angel. Keep looking ahead,' an icy, precise and slow voice ordered from behind.

Angel maintained his grip on the driver's arm.

The man wriggled. 'Can I have my arm back, before it drops off?'

'Please let go of him, Mr Angel,' the man from the back seat said coldly.

'Let go of my head and I'll think about it,' Angel replied.

'Don't turn round.'

There was a pause. The hands at his temples slackened their grip and disappeared behind him.

Angel slowly released the grip on the man's arm.

The man massaged it and exercised his fingers.

Angel said, 'What is this? Who are you? What do you want?'

There was an aggressive blowing of a car horn from behind, immediately followed by several others further back.

The man with the icy voice urgently said, 'Move it, Joshua. Move it.'

Noisily, the driver selected a gear and let in the clutch. The car moved off.

Angel's brain raced.

'Who are you and what do you want?' he bawled.

'Forgive this unorthodox approach, Mr Angel, but secrecy is absolutely paramount. I'm Harry Youel. You may have heard of me.'

Angel's stomach somersaulted. Half the forces in the country were looking for him. 'No,' he lied. 'What do you want? I must warn you. I am a police officer and this is a hijack.' He pointed a thumb over his shoulder. 'And what about that accident?'

'It's nothing. A broken light cover. Joshua will sort it out. Won't you Joshua?'

'Yes, Mr Youel,' the big man said.

Youel continued, 'This is not a hijack. We are providing transport to wherever you want to go. Now where is that? Just say where you want to go, and Joshua will drive you there, won't you Joshua?'

'Yes Mr Youel,' the man said agreeably.

Angel thought quickly; it wouldn't be a bright idea to take this trio home with him. 'The police station on Church Street,' he said firmly.

'Did you get that, Joshua?'

'Yes, Mr Youel.'

'Now while Joshua is working on that, you and I can have a word.'

The car moved out of the traffic and up the hill.

Angel sniffed. 'I don't think we'll have much in common.'

'It's about my son, Sebastian, Mr Angel.'

'Don't think I know him.'

'Well, it is like this, Mr Angel,' Youel said icily. 'You police have to leave my son alone. I cannot do with you interfering in his life. He's a delicate young man and he needs nurturing and encouraging. He will not be able to blossom with heavy boots tramping all round him. So I want you to leave him alone. I have great plans for him. Let him develop. At present, he's only a sapling; I want him to grow into an oak tree. So keep away from him. Give him air to breathe; room to expand.'

'You mean, let him do as he likes,' Angel said drily.

Youel's voice hardened. 'I mean it, Mr Angel. And I have the power and the will to see that it is carried out. Name your price.'

'Eh? Price for what?'

'Price to get that stupid misunderstanding at that super-market cash machine sorted out.'

'Oh, *that's* your son,' Angel said cagily. 'I couldn't do it if I wanted to. It's not my case. Besides, there's CCTV proof that he was an accomplice to the copying of a credit card.'

'How much for the tape?'

'I haven't got it. I haven't even access to it. It's with the CPS.'

'Get it.' A hand with a small brown paper packet appeared by his right ear. 'In this wrapper is a thousand pounds.'

Angel shook his head firmly. 'I couldn't possibly. Even if I wanted to.'

The hand shot back and reappeared with three brown paper packets.

'Three thousand pounds.'

'No.'

'Look Mr Angel, I am talking to you in a moving car so that we can't be overheard, nobody at Bromersley nick or anywhere else will ever know we've even met. No notes, no memos, no minutes, no wires. It looks innocent enough, doesn't it? Four men in a car, chatting. We might be talking about women or football.'

Angel rubbed his chin. 'Yes,' he said angrily. 'Well, what are we *really* talking about?'

'*Ten* thousand pounds.'

Angel's eyes bounced; his pulse throbbed more loudly in his ears. 'It can't be done, even if I wanted to take your money.'

'Everybody can use money, Mr Angel. Think of what you can buy with ten thousand pounds. Think of the women you can get ... they'll be all over you like flies ... and the coke or H or whatever you're into.'

'I don't want your money, Mr Youel.'

'You will ... you will ... one day. In the meantime, Mr Angel, leave my son alone and tell all your friends to leave him alone too. Remember, anything that belongs to Harry Youel stays with Harry Youel, and is protected by Harry Youel's personal protection plan. You will come to learn that I am a one-man insurance company, Mr Angel. Everything I own and everybody who works for me is covered by a fully comprehensive policy; it has my personal guarantee of protection from every kind of ... disturbance. And the cover and the service apply twenty-four hours a day, seven days a week. The premiums are *very* reasonable and the service is matchless. Isn't that right, Joshua?'

'Yes, Mr Youel,' the driver replied looking briefly back from the windscreen.

'Isn't that right, Poodle?'

'Yes, Mr Youel,' a voice from the back seat replied.

'And claims are always paid out promptly ... generously ... with a bonus.'

'Hmm. And how do clients contact you then?' Angel said, running his tongue round his mouth.

'Ah, yes. There's the difference, Mr Angel. There's the big difference. My clients don't contact me: I contact them. They don't choose me: I choose them.'

Joshua turned the car left into Church Street. Youel said, 'We're nearly at your destination, Mr Angel. What's it to be? This is a never-to-be-repeated offer. Ten thousand pounds and a lifetime guarantee of personal protection ... no more falling down stone steps ... or your car exploding when you come out of church ... or your wife being kidnapped on a supermarket car park ... or you being framed for something you didn't do ... I'm offering you a go-anywhere, anytime, do-anything policy. And the premium is so cheap ... All you have to do is get my son off this mistaken identity charge, and then we could see what the future might hold for you. Now what do you say?'

Angel shook his head. This was a tricky moment.

The car stopped.

'We're here already, Mr Angel,' Youel said. 'It's make-your-mind-up time.'

He was amazed to be returned to the station in one piece. 'My mind is made up. It's thanks, but no thanks.'

There was a pause.

'I'll keep in touch,' Youel snarled. 'Rest assured, I am *never* far away.'

Angel licked his lips as he reached for the door handle. He would be glad to get away from this mob.

'Help the inspector out, Poodle. Where are your manners?' Youel chided.

The giant heaved himself out of the seat; the springs relaxed and the near side of the car rose two inches.

'Goodbye for now, Mr Angel. I'll be in touch. By the way, when you get out, don't look back,' Youel said icily.

Poodle ran round the car and opened the front passenger door.

Angel got a very close look at him as he pulled himself out of the seat. He had a head like a pig mounted on a pillar from Stonehenge, draped in a navy blue serge suit with a button-up waistcoat.

Angel straightened up and stood uncertainly on the pavement; he needed the crutches. They had been on the back seat. He peered into the car, ignoring Youel's threat. There wasn't much of the little man visible; he was wearing a brown trilby hat and a scarf covered his mouth, chin and ears. His eyes shone like small, black marbles; nothing seemed to be alive behind them.

The window instantly opened two inches. 'Don't stare at me!' Youel screamed through the gap, his eyes blazing. 'Poodle!' he snarled.

'Yes Mr Youel,' he said still holding the door.

'Reward him,' he said and the window quickly closed.

Angel looked up at the giant. He wondered what Youel had meant.

Poodle slammed the car door, turned, grabbed Angel by his lapels, pulled him up close so that his snout almost touched Angel's nose, then thrust him away backwards with great power towards a privet hedge. Angel shot over it into a border of spent daffodils and tulips. He rolled over again and came to rest on his back in the middle of a flowerbed. He pulled a painful face and took a deep breath.

He heard Youel's chilling voice call out, 'Get in, you fool.' Then, a door slammed, the engine revved and the car raced off.

He eased himself up on his elbows, pulled a face and rubbed his side, but he was mostly worried about his knee. He must get to his feet. He wanted that car number. He rolled on to his side. Then he heard the squeal of brakes, the grating of gears, the sound of the engine revving. The car had reversed back. What now? There was the clatter of metal on the road. It was his crutches. They had been thrown through the car window. There was another painful grating from the gearbox, followed by more loud revving from the engine, a squeal of tyres and then silence.

He struggled to his feet.

A lady passing by, carrying two plastic bags of shopping, stopped and retrieved the crutches from the road.

Angel dusted down his front, ran a hand over his hair and straightened the hanging of his coat. He picked his way precariously around the privet hedge.

'Are you all right?' the lady enquired.

'Yes thanks.'

'These yours?' she said offering him the crutches.

'Aye. Thank you,' he said taking them from her and placing them under his arms. He felt better when his hands tightened round the grips and he could feel the rubber feet supporting him safely on the pavement.

'My!' she said. 'Disgraceful behaviour. I should report it to the police. The station's just here, look.'

He sighed. 'Ta. I think I will,' he said making for the bottom step up to the front door.

Angel scaled the stone steps with crutches in record time, and raced through reception and down the green corridor to the CID office. 'Ahmed,' he called, breathing heavily. 'Has the super gone?'

'Yes.' The young man's jaw dropped open as he looked at the red face. 'Are you all right, sir? Can I get you anything?'

'Aye. Get me the FSU, urgently.'

'Yes sir,' he said still staring bewildered at him.

'Is there an obbo on Littlecombe school?'

'I don't know, sir.'

'Well, crack on with that call,' he snapped. 'Then get me DI Pogle. Come on, lad, *chop chop!*'

Angel turned and rocked his way up to his own office, cast the crutches to one side and let them slither noisily on to the floor. He slumped down in the swivel chair and wiped his face with his handkerchief. A minute later, the phone rang. He reached out for it.

'FSU, sir.'

'Right, lad.' There was a click, then he said, 'DI Angel, Bromersley. Who am I speaking to?'

'DI Waldo White, Firearms Support Unit, what can I do for you?'

'I've just been hijacked by Harry Youel and two of his gang in a car in the main street here in Bromersley.'

'Harry Youel?! Hell. Are you all right? Where are you speaking from?'

'Bromersley nick. Yes. I'm all right. They were in a small red Italian car; I couldn't get the index. They drove away from here about three minutes ago.'

'Right. You *sound* all right. Do you know which direction they were heading?'

'No.'

'I'll get back to you in a couple of minutes. Just let me get the show on the road. Won't be long.'

The line went dead.

Angel replaced the handset. It rang immediately.

'I've got DI Pogle on line one, sir,' Ahmed said urgently.

'Right. Bring yourself in here, lad.' He stabbed the number. 'Hello Desmond. Are you running an obbo on that kid's school?'

'Yes. I'm speaking to you from it now. Why?'

'I've just had a run-in with Harry Youel and two of his gang in town and —'

'*What?*' He gasped. 'Are you all right?'

'Yes.'

'Didn't know he was already round here!'

'I've informed FSU, but I *haven't* told them about his son and that we have an obbo on him. Wouldn't want them turning up there and frightening Sebastian off. It would ruin any chance we might have of netting his father.'

'Oooh,' Pogle muttered. 'Er. That's right. What's the super say?'

Angel wanted to dodge that one. The super would be at home watching football (or something) on the telly, and he reckoned that what the super didn't know, wouldn't do him any harm.

'He's not here,' Angel said. 'Well if you can keep the obbo running a few more days, Youel just might walk straight in to see his son. Then *you* could call in the FSU,' he said feigning optimism. 'The collar would be down to you and you'd be the super's blue-eyed boy, wouldn't you?'

Angel waited, he hoped he had persuaded him.

Pogle took a few moments to reply, then he spoke enthusiastically. 'Yes, well, I suppose I can keep it going a few more days. I've got a little shelter on a platform in a tree organized. It's about two hundred and fifty yards from the house. It's a bit exposed to the elements and there are no mod cons, but it's a perfect spot to see both the front door and the side door. Nothing can get past me.'

Angel smiled. 'Sounds great. Good luck.' He replaced the phone still beaming.

Ahmed came in, his eyes shining with anticipation.

'Have Gawber and Crisp gone home?' Angel snapped.

'Don't know, sir. They were on the door-to-door.'

'Hmmm.' The phone rang again. He picked up the handset. 'Angel.'

'Waldo White. We are on our way. We're pulling out of the yard now. I am leading a squad of four in two four-by-fours. We'll be there in twenty minutes. We need a starting point. Where did you last see them?'

Angel said, 'I was dumped out of their car right outside the station, ten minutes ago.'

'That was brazen. I've got ARVs taking up positions on the M1 and the A1, monitoring both directions, on the assumption they are leaving the area. I've told them to look for three men in a small red Italian car, that's all I've got. In the absence of any leads, we'll do the hotels, guesthouses and every other place of accommodation in and around Bromersley.'

7

The following morning, Angel arrived in his office at 8.28 a.m. The phone was already ringing. He dropped the crutches and reached over the desk for it. 'Angel.'

It was the superintendent. He didn't sound happy. 'There's a signal on my desk from the FSU. Did you call them out last night?'

'Yes sir.'

'I should have been advised,' he growled. 'What happened?'

'You'd already left, sir,' Angel said and he told him about the ambush by Harry Youel, the offer of a bribe, the skirmish outside the front of the station and his subsequent action of summoning the FSU.

'You were assaulted by an east end gangster and you chose not to tell me anything about it?' Harker bawled.

Angel held the phone away from his ear, then he said, 'I was coming in to tell you about it, first thing.'

'First thing? *This is first thing!*' he ranted. 'What happened then?'

'I didn't know you were in, sir. They found nothing, so the DI called everything off at 0045 hours, and phoned me.'

'Hmmm,' he grunted. 'Well, next time you call FSU out, I want to be told about it … *when* it happens, not twelve hours later. Right?'

'Right.'

The phone went dead.

Angel replaced the handset and pulled a face. He was thinking it was a bad start to the day. He picked up the crutches, stashed them in the corner, then shuffled his way to the swivel chair. He flopped into it and dragged the pile of post across to the middle of the desk and began fingering through it.

There was a knock at the door.

'Come in.'

It was Ahmed. 'Good morning, sir.'

'What is it, lad?' Angel growled impatiently without looking up.

'There's a gentleman in reception to see you,' he began. 'Well, no sir, not exactly to see you.'

Angel looked up. His jaw stiffened. 'Eh? Come on lad, don't talk in riddles. What are you on about? Does he want to see me or doesn't he?'

Ahmed coughed. 'I'm sure he'd *like* to see you, sir, but he *can't* because he's blind.'

Angel paused. His face brightened. 'Oh? You mean the blind witness, Mr Mountjoy?'

'Yes sir. He's here with his blind dog.' He stopped again. 'I don't mean his *dog* is blind, sir. Mr Mountjoy is blind. The dog can see, but —'

'Oh, give it a rest, Ahmed,' Angel said impatiently. 'Show him in … and his dog.'

Three minutes later, Ahmed knocked at the door and there stood Mr Mountjoy, a well-dressed man in his fifties, dark brown moustache, wearing sunglasses, a light-coloured raincoat and trilby hat and carrying a white-painted wooden walking stick. He was accompanied by a cream-coloured Labrador dog strapped in an aluminium and plastic yellow dayglo harness.

Angel stood up. 'Come in, Mr Mountjoy.'

'Good morning, you must be Inspector Angel,' the man said holding a hand out into space.

Angel found it and gave him a warm handshake. The dog wagged its tail and he reached down and rubbed its head.

Ahmed helped the man to the chair nearest the desk and the dog settled on the floor.

'Thank you for coming in, Mr Mountjoy. I was coming to see you. We are so busy; it was just a matter of time.'

'Now that's what I've got plenty of, inspector,' he said with a smile.

Angel understood, and nodded sympathetically. 'Yes, well now, tell me about last Tuesday.'

'Yes. I was passing the front of the flats where that poor woman, Mrs Drabble, was murdered. I go to my sister-in-law's for lunch every day. My brother and his wife live at the other side of the estate and it's a good walk for my dog. I had passed the flats and crossed the road to go into the recreation ground. When I was through the gates, a car roared up to me from the car park. I thought it was going to hit me. The driver angrily pipped the horn and —'

'How do you know he pipped the horn *angrily*?'

'Because of the pattern: three short pips and a long blast, followed by another long blast. Even-tempered people seeing my white stick and dog would have stopped, not pipped their horn at all, and waited until I had gotten out of the way.'

Angel nodded. 'What happened then?'

'The car reversed, revving unnecessarily high, another indication of the disposition of the driver, and then pulled forward and away with a slight squeal of the tyres.'

'Hmm.'

'It was a three-litre petrol-driven engine.'

Angel's eyebrows went up. 'How do you know that?'

'Because of the sound of the acceleration from the static position. And petrol exhaust is more smoky and sweeter than diesel.'

'Mmm. And what makes you think it might have been the murderer in the car?'

'My brother said that it was the most likely place to choose to park a car if you didn't want it to be seen outside the flats. And, according to the newspaper, the time fits exactly. It was about two o'clock, wasn't it?'

Angel smiled. 'Your brother should be a policeman. My sergeant says you would be able to recognize the car if you heard it again.'

'If I heard the car engine from the static position worked through the gears, yes, I would.'

'One last thing, Mr Mountjoy. Do you think the driver of that car realized that you are blind?'

He smiled. 'I've never met anyone outside the house who saw me and thought I could see, inspector,' he said firmly.

Angel nodded in agreement. 'Thanks very much, Mr Mountjoy.'

'I hope my evidence will be helpful in catching the murderer. You can call me as a witness, if you think I can help.'

'Thank you.' Angel frowned. 'Now, how are you going to get back home?'

'My brother brought me. He'll take me back.'

Angel summoned Ahmed and instructed him to escort Mr Mountjoy and his dog back to reception.

As the door closed, Angel rubbed his chin and smiled. It wasn't often a blind man came forward and offered to be a witness! He was about to apply himself to the morning's post when the phone rang. He grunted and reached out for it. 'Angel.'

It was the superintendent. 'Come down here.'

'Right, sir,' Angel replied. It didn't sound like a friendly call. They never were these days. He sighed and reached out for the crutches.

He was outside the superintendent's door in a minute.

'Aye. Come in,' Harker growled. 'Sit down.' He continued grinding his teeth as he watched Angel manoeuvring the crutches round the door and then closing it. 'Still on them things?' he said with a sniff.

'I'll probably manage without them next week. I'm due at the hospital on Tuesday for a check-up. They might take the dressing off. It depends whether the cartilage has —'

The super interrupted. 'It's taking an awful long time, lad,' he said with another sniff.

'Now regarding last night ... it was Harry Youel who ambushed you?'

'Yes sir.'

'Did he rough you up? What did he want?'

'No, not really, sir. He wanted to put me on his payroll and make a contribution to my pension fund.'

Harker did a bit more grinding. 'Hmm. How much?'

'Ten thousand pounds.'

The thick ginger eyebrows shot up. 'Hell fire! His rates have gone up more than inflation!' He ground a bit more and then sniffed. 'Were they armed?'

'Didn't see anything, but I suspect they were. He had two heavies with him. Both bruisers. A man called Joshua and an Irishman he called Poodle. And there was a young lad who called himself Smith. He just drove a car, I think.'

'You were damned lucky to get away from him in one piece,' the superintendent bawled and then ground some more corn. 'Now we've got the *niceties* out of the way, I want to know what you're doing about these Sanson-Drabble murders. Are you anywhere near making an arrest? Or is it beyond you ... with those crutches and so on? Do you want me to hand it over to Pogle?'

Angel involuntarily sucked in a quick short breath. His fists tightened as his fingernails cut into the palms of his hands. He didn't think much of Desmond Pogle at the best of times, and he certainly wasn't agreeable to have him take over the case. The idea filled him with horror. 'I can handle it, sir,' he said firmly. 'Anyway, I thought Pogle was busy up a tree out at that school in Littlecombe?'

The superintendent raised his bushy eyebrows again and gawped at him for a second in surprise, but he didn't respond to the comment. 'Well, just review the case for me. Tell me what you are doing? Who your suspects are? What's your strategy?'

Angel had to confess he hadn't any suspects and there wasn't any strategy. He licked his lips. 'The essence of the case, sir, is that somebody appears to be looking for something ... something to do with the Ogmores or Ogmore Hall.'

'What do you mean? A letter, a testament, a will, deeds to the Hall, what you talking about?'

'Don't know, sir ... Sanson was the butler, Mrs Drabble the housekeeper ... and they've both had their personal possessions searched through. Lady Emerald's house has also been turned over. Sanson and Drabble were murdered, presumably because they were obstructing the murderer's search. The murderer has left no prints, no DNA, nothing. Both murders were committed by the insertion of stilettos straight into the heart. The stilettos were left in the victims and are identical weapons. In the case of Sanson only, there was some recent bruising to the stomach. Mac says that was the result of being punched several times by clenched fists. The only lead I have is a witness of the car that was probably used by the murderer of Mrs Drabble, but —'

The superintendent suddenly stopped grinding his teeth and looked up. 'What's this? I don't know about this. This is new. It's a valuable lead, lad. What have you done about it?'

'Well, nothing yet, sir. You see the witness is blind.'

The superintendent pulled a face longer than a stick of rhubarb. '*Blind!*' he bawled. '*Blind!* What the hell is the use of a blind witness?'

Angel knew he was on weak ground. 'I don't know. That's why I haven't mentioned it.'

'I should think you haven't. Is *that* your only clue?'

'Yes.'

'I think you're losing your marbles, lad. I can see you are desperate, but that's ridiculous!'

Angel stood there looking as if his fly was undone. He couldn't think of anything to say.

The superintendent wrinkled his nose and then said, 'Well, *who* are your suspects then?'

'I haven't got any. I won't have until I know what the murderer is looking for.'

The super shook his head. 'What the hell are you doing all day then? Gazing into your crystal ball?'

'Legwork, sir. Traditional police work. Interviewing witnesses. Gathering information.'

'You mean hoping for the best!'

'No! I'm awaiting Dr Mac's PMs on Sanson and Drabble, also to see if there is any forensic. And I'm awaiting reports from Gawber, Crisp and Scrivens regarding their interviews with people present at the auctioneer's at the time of Sanson's murder. When I have the manpower, I intend to look into the background of the two murdered people. I am looking for other employees of the Ogmores, particularly Kate Cumberland, secretary to the late Lord Ogmore. I fear she may possibly be in grave danger.'

The superintendent looked as if his haemorrhoids were being examined with a knife and fork. 'Right. Well you'd better get back to it then. All this blather is just wasting time.'

Angel let him have the last word. He rocked his way angrily back up to his office and was met at the door by Ahmed who followed him into his office.

'Now lad, what is it?' he said as he lowered himself into the chair.

'I've got some good news and some bad news, sir.'

Angel glared at him. 'It's not time for parlour games, lad. Give us the bad news first, then at least I know I've got *summat* good to look forward to.'

'Well sir, you wanted me to find a woman called Sagar aged between sixty-six and seventy-eight? Well, I haven't been able to. I've been through the phone book and cross-checked it with the electoral roll. There are eleven Sagars listed, but they are all much younger. There's one in Welham Crescent, who is fifty. She'd be the nearest.'

He shook his head. 'She's no good; the age doesn't fit. The woman I am looking for is Cyril Sagar's widow. She's got to be about seventy now.' He sniffed. 'She may have remarried, in which case her name *wouldn't* be Sagar.' Angel sighed. 'Hmm. Looks like we'll have to do it the hard way. Go back to the records and find Sagar's last address.'

Ahmed nodded.

'And there's something else. I want you to go down to the Bromersley Chronicle office. If you ask them nicely, they might let you look at past issues dated around August 1962. A copper taking his own life would be bound to be well covered ... probably on the front page ... See if you can get any info about his widow ... her name ... where she worked, *if* she worked. Something to act on. And keep it stum, lad. Understand?'

Ahmed nodded knowingly. It sounded as if it might be interesting, and proper detective work ... out of the office.

'Now what's the good news?'

'Kate Cumberland has turned up, sir.'

Angel's mouth opened. His face brightened. 'Kate Cumberland? Mmm.' Then he asked quickly, 'Is she alive?'

'Alive and well.'

Angel smiled, then he frowned and shook his head. He rubbed the lobe of his ear between his thumb and forefinger while looking closely at Ahmed. 'Her place *has* been turned over?'

'Yes, sir.'

He nodded. 'I'd better get there, right away. I'll want transport. Get me Ron Gawber. And pass me those crutches. What's the address?'

Twenty minutes later, Gawber and Angel were on their way out of Bromersley. They went on Huddersfield Road, down the hill and round the Victoria Falls roundabout with its fountain of water tumbling elegantly down the marble steps. Up the hill, they went past the Ogmore Hall gates, past Littlecombe school on their left. About two miles after that, they pulled into a short unmade lane in the middle of nowhere, off the main Huddersfield Road. There were four terraced houses standing 90 degrees to the main thorough-fare. An unmarked police car was parked outside the farthest one. Gawber drove down the lane and pulled up beside it.

Angel swung his way on the crutches up to the snicket gate. Gawber opened it and they made their way to the little front door and knocked on it.

DC Todd opened the door. 'Oh, it's you, sir.'

They exchanged nods.

The young man pulled the door open wide. 'Been expecting you. SOCOs have been and gone. It's all yours. DI Pogle said I was to stay here until you arrived.'

'Of course, he's very busy on a job,' Angel said slyly.

Todd licked his lips. 'I believe he is, sir,' he replied, careful not to be specific.

Angel smiled. Then he glanced round; the room was a mess, a sight that was becoming depressingly repetitive. His face changed to gloom. The floor was covered with furnish-ings, ornaments and domestic clutter of every sort, savagely strewn from cupboards, drawers, table and the mantelpiece. What was the need for it? he asked himself.

'Did SOCOs find anything useful, lad?'

'Don't think so, sir. They didn't indicate any great find. They said the intruder wore gloves.'

Angel nodded. 'Anything taken?'

'The owners didn't seem to think so.'

'Where are they? *Who* are they?'

'A young couple: Kate Cumberland and Nicholas Magson. They're both teachers at the local school. They've been up and then gone back. It's only a small school. The children couldn't be left. They'll be back again at dinnertime.'

'Right.' Angel turned to Gawber. 'Same MO.'

Gawber nodded. 'Looks like it.'

He turned back to Todd. 'Any idea when the break-in occurred?'

'Between a quarter to nine and ten o'clock, sir. They left for school together about eight forty-five. The next-door neighbour reported it at 1010 hours. Saw a window at the back broken. Didn't see anybody though.'

'They never do. Have a look round, Ron, and have a word next door,' he said leaning forward on the crutches.

Gawber picked his way over the papers and stuff on the floor of the tiny living-room to the only door, which led to the staircase and the rest of the house.

Todd said, 'If you don't want me, sir, I'll be off. DI Pogle is expecting me.'

'Aye, get off, lad. Where's the key?'

'Just drop the latch, sir.'

'Right.'

Todd went out and closed the door. He came back a few moments later. 'I met the post lady; she gave me these, sir.' He pushed some letters into Angel's hand. 'You won't mind passing them on, sir?'

He closed the door.

Angel looked through the envelopes. One had a bold strapline above the address that read, 'You've won £10,000'. Another offered '35% off a wheelchair of your choice'. There was a brown envelope that looked like a gas bill, and also one elegant, handwritten, thick cream envelope. He peered with interest at the latter. It was addressed to Miss Kate Cumberland and postmarked 3 May. At the top of the envelope in small gilt lettering was printed: 'From Ogmore Hall, Bromersley, South Yorkshire.' Holding the letters, he pursed his lips and looked thoughtfully through the cottage window at nothing in particular. The sound of footsteps disturbed his thoughts; he turned to see Gawber, picking his way through the rubble.

'Nothing new. Nothing different, sir. It's like the others. It's a tip upstairs. Whatever they were looking for, they certainly made a thoroughly bad job of looking for it.' He sighed. 'Had a word with the lady next door. She saw nothing and heard nothing. She came out to hang some washing on the line and noticed she was walking on glass.'

Angel sniffed. He placed the envelopes in the middle of the bare dining table.

'It's gone twelve. Take me back to the station. You can come back here and have a word with Kate Cumberland and Nicholas Magson later.'

They dropped the latch and returned to the car.

Gawber drove the car down the bumpy lane and rejoined the main road to Bromersley. They were only two miles from Littlecombe school. The road was busy: there were a few live-stock vehicles, some delivery vans and several cars in convoy travelling towards town. As they approached Littlecombe, Angel noticed a small red car coming towards them. It suddenly turned left and drove through the stone gates of the school and disappeared out of sight. It was there and gone in two seconds; but in that time, Angel had managed to see that there were three people in it, and that the man in the front passenger seat was wearing a hat and a scarf covering the lower half of his face. He gasped as he realized it was Harry Youel and his two heavies, Joshua and Poodle. His eyes lit up. *They had driven straight into Pogle's trap*! A shiver of excitement ran down his spine.

'Did you see that, Ron?' he gasped elatedly.

'What, sir?'

'That car. Turned into Littlemore school.'

'I saw a blue van, way back ...'

'No. No. A red car. A little red car.'

'No sir.'

'That was Harry Youel and his troupe of performing seals,' he said. 'They've walked straight into Pogle's trap!' He smiled. His mind raced. What a coup. Youel off the streets after all these years. The super would be delighted. It was about time something went right. 'It should only take about twenty minutes for the FSU to get there,' he said to Gawber nodding with pleasure.

'It's a big, big collar for DI Pogle,' Gawber replied. 'Should we go back and give him a hand?'

'No. If we were seen, it might blow the gaff. No. Let's not take any risks. Let him have his day of glory.' He sniffed and added smugly, 'He's due for one.'

Gawber smiled.

They arrived at the station a few minutes later. Angel scrambled out of the car and made for the steps up to the front door. Gawber reversed into the station yard to turn round and make his way back to Kate Cumberland's cottage.

Angel rocked his way through reception and down the corridor.

Ahmed spotted him and ran into the office after him. 'There's some photographs from SOC on your desk, sir. And Dr Mac's been on the phone.'

Angel nodded. He handed the crutches to him and then pointed to the phone. 'Get him back for me,' he said as he slumped down in the swivel chair.

Ahmed stacked the crutches in the corner, walked over to the desk and picked up the phone.

Angel glanced at the twenty or so 10" x 8" photographs on the desk and ran a hand over his chin. He fingered through them. They were shots of the murder scene at Drabble's flat, Sanson's house and Lady Emerald's house taken by SOCO. Except for the excessive amount of blood at Drabble's flat, they all looked pretty much the same: an unruly spread of jumble.

'Can I ask you something about those photographs, sir?' Ahmed said as he dialled. 'Aye. What is it, lad?'

A voice down the line said, 'Dr Mac.' Ahmed passed him the phone.

'Michael Angel. You rang me, Mac?'

'Aye. Only to say I've finished the PM on that Sanson chap. I can confirm that he suffered two contusions to the lower abdomen, and two to the liver, but they did not contribute to his death. I believe all four blows would have been delivered by a man or men with clenched fists. Also, he must have been quite a drinker; his liver had seen better days.'

'Oh? Right. Thank you, Mac. Anything else unusual … of use to me? Anything under the fingernails? Under his shoes? Tattoos? Was he a drug user? Needle marks? Foreign contents in the stomach? You know what I'm looking for.'

'Negative to all those, Mike. Looked like a regular chap who enjoyed life, perhaps a bit too well. I'll send the full SP and his personal effects over first thing on Monday.'

'Right. Thanks. What about Alison Drabble?'

'Tuesday, I reckon.'

'Right. Thanks Mac. Goodbye.'

Angel replaced the phone and rubbed his chin.

Ahmed began, 'My question, sir …'

'Oh, yes lad?'

'I've heard you say several times that the person who searched Mr Sanson's, Mrs Drabble's and Lady Ogmore's homes was an amateur. Well sir, the photographs show the houses to be an absolute mess. How can you tell it was an amateur?'

Angel looked at Ahmed and smiled. 'Good question. Now, if you were a house burglar, you'd want to be in and out of that house as fast as you possibly could, wouldn't you? Obviously, the longer you are there, the more risk there is of you being caught. The faster you work, the less likely you are to finish up in Armley. Now, an amateur approaching a chest of drawers would open the top drawer, rummage through it, close it and move down to the second drawer, look through that, close it and move down to the next drawer and so on down to the bottom. A professional thief would start at the bottom, pull out the drawer, rummage through it, leave it open and move up to the next drawer, rummage through that, leave that open and move upwards to the next drawer and so on to the top, leaving all the drawers hanging open. That way the professional has saved a few seconds.'

Ahmed stood there with his mouth open.

Angel said, 'Now look at these photographs. The intruder in this case has consumed or wasted even more time; the drawers have been pulled out off their runners and the contents tipped out. You'll notice the top drawer has been searched first, because it is at the bottom of the pile and the bottom drawer is at the top!'

Ahmed nodded in admiration.

'Now pass me those crutches.' He reckoned Pogle would have reported in by now. FSU would be in charge at Littlecombe school. Harry Youel would be in handcuffs. He must find out what's happening.

He rocked down the corridor and knocked on the superintendent's door.

'Come in,' Harker bawled.

'What's the latest then, sir? Have FSU got Harry Youel?'

The super's ginger eyebrows arched upwards. He took in a deep breath. 'Don't know what you're talking about,' he snapped.

'Coming back from an enquiry ... about half-an-hour ago, I saw Youel and two men in a car turn into Littlecombe school. That obbo is *still* on there, isn't it?'

The superintendent didn't reply. Angel could see realization dawning on Harker's lined face. He stared back at Angel with glazed eyes and reached out to pick up the phone. He had to look down to dial the number. Angel could hear it ringing out.

There was a click and then he quickly said, 'Pogle? ... Everything all right, lad? ... Anything to report? ... Harry Youel turned up? ... *No*? Are you sure? ... Three men in a red car?'

Superintendent Harker glared at Angel; he looked as happy as a bus driver with a boil on his bum. He turned back to the phone. 'No? ... Right. Has *anybody* arrived in the last hour or so? ... No? Right ... No. Stay where you are.'

He replaced the handset.

'I think you're going round the twist, lad. Or you need glasses! Was Ron Gawber with you when you saw this — car?'

'I didn't make a mistake, sir. I saw the car and I saw Harry Youel in a hat with his face half-covered, which was how he was yesterday.'

'If his face was half-covered, how do you know it was him? It could have been anybody.'

'Not with those two passengers; not in an identical red car.'

'Was it the same index number?'

'I didn't get the index number.'

'Well, how do you know it was the same car, then?!' he growled angrily.

'It was.'

'And did Gawber see this ... this invisible car?'

'No.'

'I'm not surprised. Pogle says nobody's called at the place all morning. And certainly not a car with Harry Youel in it!'

8

'I've something to show you, love,' Mary said as soon as he got through the door.

'What's for tea, lass? Is it salmon?'

'Yes. Look at that old photograph album on the table. I've left it open at a page.' Angel draped the crutches over the settee and flopped into a chair at the table while loosening his tie and the top button of his shirt. He looked at the album. His eyebrows shot up and he smiled. 'Hmm. It's my mum and dad's wedding.'

Mary came out of the kitchen, walked over to the table and leaned over his shoulder. 'And there's your aunt Kate,' she pointed with a wet finger.

'Mmmm. In that funny hat. What about it?'

'What's that she has in her hand?' she asked pointedly.

He looked closely and he could see clearly the old lady posing grandly on the church steps holding a slim black cane that reached down three inches from a bridesmaid's white shoe. 'Oh, aye,' he said in surprise.

'I told you,' Mary said confidently. 'There are five or six other earlier photographs with Aunt Kate on. And she's always leaning on that stick.' She reached over his shoulder and turned over a few pages. 'Look. There's one there taken at Skegness, walking on the front. She must have been about thirty. She's walking with a stick there, look.'

'All right, love. You've made your point. So she had a stick. She *always* had a stick.'

Mary shook her head. 'For a detective, you're a bit slow sometimes.'

'Thank you. That's twice today I've been told off.'

She smiled softly. 'Oh. Mr Charm been having a go at you?'

He sniffed. 'The point is, how would anybody else *know* that she needed a stick?'

'You don't believe the obvious, do you?'

'This latest photograph was taken over forty years ago. She died in 1962. Half the world wasn't born then.'

'And half the world has died since. And those that are left didn't know Aunt Kate and couldn't have cared less whether she had a stick or not,' she said turning away to the kitchen.

'That's why it's a mystery! If the explanation was obvious, I wouldn't be looking for a solution, would I? It's so aggravating. It *isn't* obvious. I have to find out how Selina Bailey knew.'

'She's a medium. She can see these things,' Mary called impatiently. 'She has a gift to see the past. Some people have! It isn't new. There have been mediums around for hundreds of years.'

'And there have been confidence tricksters around since time began!'

He turned back the few pages in the album to the photograph of his parents' wedding.

'It's nearly ready,' Mary called angrily from the kitchen. 'Will you lay the table or not?'

'Aye,' he muttered.

He lifted the photograph out of the page and turned it over. At the bottom corner was a little gilt label with the words 'Gorman Photographers' in black stuck on to it. He shook his head. He'd heard the name before; it was an old, respected family business from years ago. He remembered the name had appeared on the back of photographs of him as a baby. He heard the rattle of plates from the kitchen.

'I'm bringing it in,' Mary called.

*

It was 8.28 a.m. Monday, 9 May, when Angel arrived at the station. He rocked his way down the corridor to his office, slung the crutches into a corner, hung his coat on the hook on the side of the stationery cupboard and dropped into the swivel chair. He looked at the pile of post in the middle of the desk and the corners of his mouth turned down. Blowing eight inches of hot air, he began to finger through the envelopes. There was a knock at the door.

'Come in.'

It was Ahmed.

'Good morning, sir,' he said brightly.

'Huh,' Angel growled. 'What's good about it?' he replied without looking up. 'There was a time when I could do this job without getting a pain in my chest.'

'Well, for one thing, sir,' Ahmed said brightly. 'It isn't raining.'

'Mmm,' he grunted. 'It's forecast for this afternoon, lad.'

Ahmed smiled and shook his head.

Angel looked up. 'Have you just come in here to give me a weather report?'

'No sir. I've got that address you wanted ... Cyril Sagar's.'

'Ah,' he said, his face brightening. 'What is it then?' His pen was poised.

'11 Bartholomew Street.'

'Aaaah. Right,' he said scratching it out on the back of a used envelope and slipping it into his pocket.

'And I've been down to the Bromersley Chronicle office and seen all four issues for August 1962. It came out on a Saturday then, sir.'

'Aye. Did you find out anything useful about Mrs Sagar?'

'No sir. It said he left a widow and a daughter but it didn't give any names or addresses or even initials. There was nothing that would give us a lead to where they might be living now.'

Angel wrinkled his nose.

'It did mention someone who you know, though,' Ahmed said with a smile.

'Oh? Who?'

'Mrs Buller-Price, sir. She was a witness to him falling, and she was present at the coroner's inquest. *And* she was interviewed on television.'

Angel blinked. 'Now that's interesting.'

Ahmed beamed.

'You'd better phone her up and ask her if she'd be kind enough to call in here next time she's in town. Do it nicely.'

'Right, sir.'

Angel rubbed his mouth hard, then he said, 'Aye. There's something else, while I think about it. I want a list of calls made last month from 28 Huddersfield Road, that's the home of a woman who calls herself a 'medium', Selina Bailey. You can get her number from the book. And keep *that* enquiry under your hat.'

'Right, sir.'

'And where are Crisp and Scrivens?'

'Don't know, sir.'

'*Well find* out!' he snapped. 'Tell them I want to speak to them, smartish.'

'Right sir.'

There was a knock at the door. 'See who that is, lad, and then crack on. All these interruptions: this office is like Simon Cowell's audition room.'

Ahmed opened the door. It was DS Gawber.

'What is it, Ron?'

Gawber was carrying a cream file and a polythene bag with the word 'Evidence' in big red letters printed across it.

Ahmed held the door open for him and then went out.

'Just come in from Dr Mac,' Gawber said, reading the label. 'PM report on Geoffrey Sanson and the contents of his pockets.'

'Aaah,' Angel said and held out his hands. He put the stuff on the desk and began to open the plastic bag.

'Can I have a word, sir?'

Angel nodded towards the chair.

'A woman's just been in to report her husband missing. An Anton Mulholland.'

Angel looked up briefly then frowned. 'Happens every day.'

'The type of man, age and so on … it's a bit different. This chap, he's fifty, highly skilled management engineer, had a long time in hospital … and still not well … he isn't working … been very ill … disappeared last Tuesday night.'

Angel shook his head impatiently. 'It'll be the milk-woman or a lass in the post office or —'

'No. It's not like that, sir.'

He shook his head again and sighed. 'Look, Ron. I've a lot on, and I can't do with a sob story on a Monday morning.'

Gawber persisted. 'He's been in touch with her, by phone, very briefly on Wednesday night. She said that he says he's being held against his will … and he needs his pills to keep him going. She says he can't manage without them.'

Angel pursed his lips and then sniffed. 'Hmm.' He shook his head and said, 'I bet his wife is a good-looker.'

Gawber's eyebrows lifted. He nodded. 'Yes. She is actually.' He smiled. 'Yes. Adele Mulholland,' he said, savouring her name.

'Aye. Well it does sound serious. Do the best you can for her, but don't bother me with it unless you have to. I am never at my best dealing with good-looking women with problems. I'm better with ugly ones whose life is sweet.' He ran his hand over his chin. 'Have you finished all your interviews in the Sanson case?' he added quickly.

'Finished on Friday, sir. Wrote them up over the weekend. Everybody says they were looking at the auctioneer or the painting, the vital moment the man was stabbed.'

'Well somebody wasn't,' he sniffed. 'Did you trace those two men in ponytails?'

Gawber shook his head. 'No, sir.'

Angel pulled a face and tipped the contents of the polythene bag on to the desk top. There was a handkerchief, key ring, two pounds in change, ballpoint pen, wallet with various credit cards, library ticket, a single ticket to York Races in June, and a cheque book with the Northern Bank. That was what he wanted; he reached out for it and eagerly looked at the stubs. There were the expected entries for regular domestic needs, but the frequent entries to pay 'Benny Peters' sums from £20 to £100 were the entries Angel was most interested in. He pointed the stubs out to Gawber. 'Who's Benny Peters?'

Gawber shook his head. Angel thrust the cheque book into his hand. 'Go down to the Northern Bank. Find out all you can about these payments, and the state of Sanson's account.'

Suddenly, Angel's office door was thrown open. It banged back against the wall noisily and rebounded back a foot or so.

The two men looked up open-mouthed.

In the doorway was the tall lumbering figure of the superintendent, grinding his teeth and producing an excess of saliva. He held out a hand. The fingers seemed to be feeling the quality of invisible cloth.

Angel's jaw dropped. Something was wrong. Something was *very* wrong.

Gawber stood up.

The superintendent's face was whiter than a death certificate. His big ginger eyebrows projected forward giving him the hooded look of a vulture.

Angel licked his lips and stood up.

'I've just had a triple nine call,' he said breathily, his red eyes staring. He rubbed his mouth with the back of his hand. 'Doctor Sinclair and his wife ... found dead ... in their house. Get over there, smartly.'

Angel's neck and arms turned to goose-flesh.

They were the first on the scene at the large Victorian semi-detached house. It was situated in one of the few elegant tree-lined streets in the town, where in the first half of the twentieth century the professional and business leaders of the town had lived and brought up their children. Sadly, it was now relegated to lumbering, ill-maintained houses, some converted into flats, as wealthy succeeding generations had made their homes in newly built, detached houses further out of town on the perimeter of the green belt.

As Gawber and Angel got out of the car, they saw a young woman in the front garden talking to a neighbour over the garden fence. When she saw them, she came running down the short garden path to the gate, a teacup in her hand. Her drawn face told the story.

'Are you the police? ... I come and do a bit of cleaning for Mrs Sinclair, three mornings a week. I came this morning. I pressed the doorbell. No reply. I tried several times. I couldn't make them hear me. Then I walked round to the French window, they sometimes leave it open for me. As I tried the handle ...' She stopped. Her face creased, tears welled round her eyes and ran down her cheeks. She dug into a pocket searching for a tissue, then looked at the empty teacup. Bending down, she put the cup on the path, stood up, found a tissue and wiped her cheeks. 'I'm sorry.' She pointed to the path leading to the rear of the house. 'Down there ... by the door ...' She shivered and turned away from the house. 'I want to go home.'

Angel nodded. 'Yes. Yes, love. We'll take you home.'

She exploded into a heart-felt cry. Angel balanced on one leg and put an arm round her.

Gawber turned away.

A police car pulled up quietly, followed by an ambulance.

'I'll just see to these chaps, love.' He signalled to Gawber to look after her.

DS Crisp and DC Scrivens came up to him with anxious faces.

'Where the hell have you two been hiding? Never mind. Check on the doors. If they're locked, break in. Go in by the back way. Quick as you can.'

Angel squeezed the grips on the crutches and propelled himself down the path towards the back of the house.

A paramedic carrying a blanket and a small bag rushed by. 'Where's the casualty?'

'We are trying to gain entry now. I'm told there are two.'

The young man blinked.

As Angel was passing the French windows, he saw that a pane of glass approximately 6" x 6" near the handle had been tapped out. He looked down for the broken fragments.

What he saw made him gasp. Inside on the room floor, only inches from the glass door and looking straight at him, was the open-eyed staring face of a woman. The sight made him freeze on the spot. It looked like an old-fashioned pot doll with long stringy hair strewn about its face. The neck was bare. The body was wearing a voluminous long white garment of some sort. The top half of it was red ... like an explosion in a dye works. There was no doubt she was dead. On the floor surrounding her and beyond was an irregular pile of tablecloths, tipped-up cutlery, coasters and sheet music. Above lines and dots he made out the words '*1812 Overture by Tchaikovsky*'. All around her was the shambles he was becoming used to seeing. He turned away. He could hear his pulse drumming in his ears and felt unreal. The door jamb looked fuzzy. He felt a hard cold brick where his stomach had been. It was impossible to continue seeing so much death and not be affected.

An ambulanceman rushed past him. 'Excuse me.'

The sight of the man and the sound of his voice brought Angel back to reality. His eyes came back into focus and he blew out a yard of breath. Gripping his crutches, he went down the path to the back door. As he approached, he heard three heavy bangs at one-second intervals, followed by the splintering of wood.

A voice said, 'We're in.'

Crisp pushed at the door several times, against some obstruction on the room floor, until the gap was wide enough for a man to get through.

'Let the medics in first,' he heard himself call out.

Crisp and Scrivens pulled away from the door. The two men in green and yellow dashed inside.

Angel looked through the open splintered door into the kitchen. The floor round the doorway was littered with packets of sugar, rice and breakfast cereals, cutlery, newspapers, the wall clock, even a broken willow-pattern roast joint dish and other kinds of domestic bits and pieces. Against the far wall he could see a big white cupboard with its doors open and empty shelves except for a solitary blue cup on the middle one. It was sickening. It was a repeat performance. How many more times?

Another vehicle arrived.

Gawber came up to him. 'That girl's in a bit of a state,' he said quietly. 'She'd be better in hospital.'

'Aye.' Angel nodded. He looked behind him. 'Scrivens,' he called.

'Yes sir.'

'There's a lass round at the front in a red coat. She found the body. The shock has got to her. Take her to the hospital urgently. Ask them to have a look at her. Wait with her. Find out if she's any family. If they discharge her, take her home. See she's all right, then come back here.'

'Right, sir.'

'And, Scrivens! Get her name and address, and if she wants to talk, listen to her, she might say something useful, but don't press her.'

He nodded, and together with Gawber he went up to the front gate.

Dr Mac came bustling down the path. They exchanged glances and shook their heads. There was no need for niceties.

These two men had been working together at Bromersley nick for twenty years.

'The super said he thought there were *two*?' His deep Glaswegian accent seemed to suit the occasion.

'One's dead ... Mrs Sinclair,' Angel said quietly. 'Don't know for certain about the doctor.'

Mac sniffed. 'Who's inside?'

'Just the medics.'

The doctor inhaled noisily, turned and mumbled something as he made his way swiftly up the path to get kitted up.

Gawber came back with a roll of blue and white 'Do not cross' tape. He went over to Crisp, said something and they began unrolling it.

The paramedic and the ambulanceman picked their way over the stuff on the kitchen floor, out on to the back step and into the yard.

Angel advanced on them.

The ambulanceman carrying a blanket and a bag avoided everybody and rushed straight up the path towards the front gate.

The paramedic looked across at Angel. He glanced at the crutches. 'Who's in charge?'

'I am. What have we got?'

The man took a deep breath. 'Two bodies. A male, white hair, about eighty ... in a first-floor bedroom. Female, presumably his wife, in that first room, ground floor ... both stabbed in the chest. Can't do anything for them. Sorry.'

*

'They were both stabbed in the heart with stilettos like Geoffrey Sanson and Alison Drabble, sir,' Angel began. 'The doctor was stabbed in bed upstairs and Mrs Sinclair down in the drawing room. The house was then taken to pieces systematically and searched; the cupboards, drawers and shelves were all cleared and the contents dumped on the floor in the usual way. And there are no fingerprints, no footprints and no witnesses, and up to now, no DNA.'

The superintendent stopped grinding his teeth and shook his head. 'We have got to stop this wholesale blood-letting some way,' he stormed. 'The chief is breathing down my neck. I've got the national press bleating away. I have even had the Editor of the *Daily Standard* phoning me at *home*! Don't know how the hell he got my number!'

Angel wrinkled his nose and shuffled uncomfortably in the chair. He licked his lips. He had never had a serial case as gruesome as this, and one so lacking in clues. He didn't know what to say, but he knew whatever he uttered would sound like an excuse.

'How did the murderer get in?' the super growled.

'Through the French window. A pane of glass was knocked in. The key was in the lock.'

'Huh. Isn't it always? Did he come out the same way?'

'Yes, sir. With difficulty. Mrs Sinclair's body was on the floor against the door. It would have to have been pushed by somebody fairly strong to enable him to squeeze out.'

'Now that's interesting. Hmm. It takes no strength at all to slip a stiletto between the ribs, but a bit of muscle would be necessary to get out of the house. Hmm. Looks like it rules out the possibility of the murderer being a woman?'

Angel nodded. 'It looks that way, sir.'

'Why was the doctor stabbed in bed and his wife downstairs?'

'I'm guessing that she heard the noise ... the smashed window pane, maybe ... came downstairs ... went into the drawing room ... the intruder stuck the stiletto in her ... Then the murderer came upstairs, into the bedroom ... and stuck the knife into him.'

'And left a stiletto stuck in each of them?' Angel nodded. 'Yes, sir. Two stilettos.' 'Sounds like they went there armed purposefully, deliberately to —'

'*They*?' he queried. 'Are you thinking plural, sir? Are you thinking *two* men?'

The superintendent's eyebrows shot up. 'Two *big* men? Strong men to push open that French window to get out?'

Angel rubbed his chin.

'Mmmm. There is one big difference, in this case,' the superintendent said, pointing a bony finger. 'Sinclair and his wife weren't part of the Ogmore troupe.'

'No sir, but he *was* their doctor. He attended both Lord Archie and Lady Emerald … was still attending *her*.' He stopped, pursed his lips and added, 'She'll not like this. She'll not like this at all.'

'Aaaah. And it's the same MO. Have you got a motive yet? What lines of enquiry are you following?'

'I have no motive, sir. I have to get confirmation that there's no DNA, and see if the post-mortems tell us anything. SOCOs are still searching the house. They *might* come up with something.'

The superintendent went through his repertoire of face-pulling. 'Aye, and they might not.'

*

'You wanted me, sir?' DS Crisp said as he closed the door.

Angel looked up and glared at him. 'Oh. The wanderer returns. Where have you been? Taking your elephants for a stroll over the Alps? Did you run out of money, or have you come back simply because it's raining?'

'No sir,' he said, disregarding the sarcasm. 'I have only just finished the enquiries, and I know you wanted me to finish them off. And you know I had to break off this morning to attend at Dr Sinclair's house.'

'Aye. Aye. Well, you'd better go back there now and help Gawber finish off. It's a big house.'

'I got something this morning, sir.'

Angel looked up. 'Oh?'

'Yes sir. I have a witness who saw two men having a serious natter, arms waving angrily, that sort of thing, with Geoffrey Sanson, down that ginnel between the butcher's and the auctioneer's.'

'Oh?' Angel's eyes bounced. His mind raced. 'When was this?'

'Just after the auction had started. Elsie Bennett ... works at the butcher's. She was coming back after delivering something to a customer and was taking a short cut across the car park. She saw them briefly as she passed the end of the ginnel.'

Angel felt his pulse rate increase. 'Did she see either of the two men actually *assault* Sanson?'

'No. But she got a good look at them; they were quite distinctive. She'd be able to identify them if she saw them again.'

'Got a description?'

'Big, middle-aged and they both had ponytails.'

9

'Good morning, sir. Have you seen the morning papers?'

'No, Ron. Have I missed something important?'

'There's a big lump of money been taken from the Northern Bank on New Street: £600,000.'

Angel looked up from his desk. 'What? A hold-up? I hadn't heard. When was this?'

'No. Fraud. Something to do with the cash machines in the wall. They're not sure exactly when, or how. Over a period of a couple of days, I think.'

There was a knock at the door. 'Come in.'

It was Ahmed. He was carrying a copy of the local newspaper, *South Yorkshire Examiner*.

'Now then, lad?' Angel said, his mind still mulling over the cash machine fraud. 'What do you want?'

Ahmed nodded at Gawber and turned to Angel. 'Have you read this, sir?' he said and slid the paper on the desk in front of him.

Angel took in the headline and read it out loud. 'South Yorks £1.5m Bank swindle!' He pushed the paper away irritably. 'So what? *You* didn't do it, did you?' he said, pulling a stern face.

Ahmed grinned.

'Well, tell me about it. In a nutshell. What happened? I've a lot on.'

Gawber said, 'There're similar headlines, on all the papers: the locals and the nationals. The national figure runs into fifty million quid!'

Ahmed read: 'There's £320,000 missing from the Woollen Bank in Doncaster, £129,000 and £402,000 from two branches of the City, Country and Capital Bank in Sheffield, and £600,000 from the Northern Bank in Bromersley.'

Angel shook his head in surprise. 'How was it done?'

The phone rang. He reached out for it. 'Angel.'

'Aye.' It was the superintendent. 'Have you seen Pogle anywhere? Is he with you?'

'No, sir. He'll be on that obbo at Littlecombe, won't he?' Angel said slyly.

The superintendent sniffed and then replied, 'Come down here then.'

There was a click and then silence.

Angel frowned and replaced the phone. He stood up. 'I've got to go.' He reached out for the crutches. 'Ron, if you find anything interesting at Sinclair's let me know. And Ahmed, see if you can find somebody called Benny Peters. Might be a bookie. And you can leave that paper there when you've read it, if you like.'

'Right, sir.'

'And tell Scrivens I want to see him,' he bawled over his shoulder as he pointed the crutches down the corridor.

He knocked on the superintendent's door and went in. A smart, well-fed man in a suit as sharp as a stiletto was sitting opposite Harker looking serious, rich and important.

The super stopped grinding his teeth. 'This is Mr Alwoodley, local representative of the Association of UK Bankers and Deposit Takers. He represents the banking fraternity in this neck of the woods. That's right Mr Alwoodley, isn't it?' he said, oozing goodwill, with a smile that would have made Anne Robinson reach for the slop bucket.

The smart man nodded, but he wasn't smiling.

'Mr Alwoodley has already seen the chief constable and he has authorized him to address senior officers,' the super said. 'Merryweather is on leave, Ascrigg is off sick and Pogle is busy, engaged on an urgent case. That leaves just you. You'll have to fill Pogle in with the gist of it later. We are all ears, Mr Alwoodley,' he said and returned to grinding his teeth.

'Yes. Thank you, superintendent,' the man began. 'As you will have heard, gentlemen, very recently, large sums of cash have been and are still being defrauded from the banks from the ATMs, the Automatic Teller Machines, the holes in the walls that dispense cash. And you probably know the system works by the connection of the ATM to the bank's computer via a telephone line. Well, a computer geek in the States has discovered how to intercept the link, override the security regime and cause the machine to pay out unmonitored sums without limit. Essentially, it works like this. An accomplice enters a valid card and PIN in the ATM in the regular way and begins a transaction. The electrical activity generated down the line enables the crook to identify the circuit out of many thousands. He introduces a resistor at that point that counters the usual credit-limit monitoring mechanism, thus allowing the ATM to pay out cash non-stop, virtually indefinitely! This man has conducted this fraud throughout the States, raking in millions of dollars. Furthermore, he has now marketed the bug and method on a franchise basis around the world. In the UK, we know there are over thirty licensees. And the word is that in this area the so-called licensee is a man called Harry Youel.'

The superintendent and Angel exchanged the slightest of glances.

Alwoodley continued. 'As we speak, this man Youel, no doubt, will have an engineer, or more than one, installing bugs in lines willy nilly, defrauding my members of millions of pounds and, in the process, destabilizing the currency. It is obviously essential that you arrest this man immediately and charge him with fraud.'

The superintendent said, 'How do you know all this, Mr Alwoodley? About this chap Harry Youel?'

'We caught a man in Glasgow, who had been a local director in the telephone company's offices. He had been beaten and shot by the thug who had bought the licence for the Glasgow area from the American. He told one of our security investigators, just before he died. You can rely upon the source, superintendent.'

'And where do we find this chap, Harry Youel?' Angel asked tongue-in-cheek. He noticed out of his eye corner, the superintendent nodding at the question.

Alwoodley blinked and then shrugged. 'I don't know. I hoped you would know that.' The superintendent said, 'If we knew where villains were hiding, life would be much simpler, Mr Alwoodley. Hmmm. Is that it? Have you finished?'

'Not quite, if you don't mind?'

The superintendent waved him on to continue and began to suck his gums.

'The ATMs and computers are constantly being updated to avoid fraud, of course, and our members are hastily installing the necessary hardware to prevent recurrences, but it will take us another month or six weeks to have everything secure. In the meantime we are losing millions of pounds.'

Angel wrinkled his nose. 'Why don't you simply empty the machines, the ATMs, until the new safeguards are in place?'

The young man smirked and lowered his eyelids momentarily. 'If only it was that simple. Our members have interbank agreements with — among others — foreign countries to fund their nationals when they are in the UK, and they have come to depend on ATMs as a reliable method of sourcing cash, as indeed have many UK customers. It would leave users stranded, be very embarrassing and would lose us a great number of depositors if we were simply to withdraw the service. And it comes at a very bad time I might say, just when we are getting customers used to interfacing with technology.'

Angel looked at the superintendent and then back at Alwoodley. 'Well, you could close all the ATMs down for six weeks, couldn't you? And your staff could learn to interface with people again,' he said with a sniff. 'It would be very much cheaper for you!'

*

Ahmed put his head round the door. 'There's Mrs Buller-Price in reception to see you, sir. I phoned her yesterday morning for you, if you remember?'

Angel pulled a face. 'What!' He certainly needed to see her, but he wished she hadn't been so prompt. 'Right, Ahmed, show her in,' he said and began to clear up the papers on his desk.

Ahmed bobbed out leaving the door ajar.

Angel resolved to be his usual charming self, but he would have to give her short shrift. Two minutes later, he heard footsteps approaching down the corridor.

Ahmed tapped on the open door and pushed it open further. 'Mrs Buller-Price, sir,' he said with a big smile.

She rolled into the office, blinking, with her mouth making movements like a goldfish.

'How nice to see you again, Mrs Buller-Price,' Angel said. 'Thank you for coming in.' He pointed to the chair.

She homed in on him, beamed and held out a big hand. Then she sat down in the chair and lowered her walking stick with the Victorian pot handle and her big leather handbag to the floor close by her feet.

He glanced across at Ahmed, who was holding the door-knob, and said, 'Two teas, lad?'

Ahmed nodded and went out.

Looking round the little office she exclaimed, 'What a lovely room you have here, inspector. But no flowers?'

'No. The chief constable doesn't like the offices decorated with flowers.'

105

'Oh really? Oh yes. Doesn't want to soften your image, I expect,' she said with a knowing wink. 'Makes it harder to get confessions out of the punks. I get the picture,' she added with a chuckle.

Angel shook his head and smiled briefly and then, very solemnly, said, 'I wanted to ask you about a very serious matter that happened in 1962.'

She blinked. 'Of course, inspector. I will help you all I can.'

'I understand you witnessed the tragic suicide of a policeman on the motorway. A PC Cyril Sagar. I don't know if you can remember that far back.'

Her eyes shone like searchlights. 'Indeed I can. My memory of it is most vivid. I can remember things that happened in my life in the fifties and sixties better than events that happened yesterday. That business was most dreadful. I didn't actually see the man fall, but I was in the car, passing the Barnsley junction. I must have arrived a few seconds afterwards ... mmm ... there he was, a shapeless heap of clothes in the road.'

'It is not the event itself I am investigating, Mrs Buller-Price. I am trying to locate the whereabouts of the man's widow. Did you happen to meet her?'

She nodded, shaking all four chins. 'Oh yes. I met her briefly. I have no idea what happened to her.'

'Can you describe her?'

'Quite pitiful, really. A little woman with a lot of dark hair in a flowered dress. I remember the sight of her clinging to her little girl, a thin, pasty 5- or 6-year-old with skinny, white legs, in that dingy hospital corridor. She was hugging a small, bright pink fluffy toy, an elephant, I think it was. Outrageous colour, Chinese pink or cyclamen. It might have been a pony. I am not sure. Dangling on an elastic. She dropped it or pushed it behind the radiator pipes. I remember laddering a stocking, creeping about on my hands and knees with a nurse, getting it out by poking it with a splint.'

'Do you remember her name, or the name of the child?'

'No. But I would have liked to have taken the little thing home and given her a plate of beef stew and broccoli. She needed building up. Fresh air in her lungs. A month on the beach at Scarborough, ice creams and some fun with other children. Mmmm. Poor little soul.'

'You can't recollect her name?'

She pursed her lips. 'Something unusual, I feel. But no. I cannot recall it, inspector. I'm sorry.'

Angel grunted. 'Ah well.'

Ahmed arrived through the open door with two cups of tea on a tin tray. He placed the tray on the desk.

'Thank you, Ahmed,' she said with a smile as she took the cup.

He went out and closed the door.

'You are due at *my* house for tea soon, inspector, you know. I am dying to use that beautiful silver teapot I bought at the auction.'

'Oh yes. Thank you, and I am looking forward to it.'

'I am sorry to hear the tragic news about Dr Sinclair and his dear wife, Clementine. Such a lovely couple. You are dealing with that investigation, inspector?'

'I'm afraid I am.'

'And you are also investigating the murders of Mr Sanson and Alison Drabble. All those lovely people gone inside a week, and good people, I believe. All stabbed by the same silent killer, it says in the papers. Somebody local. Someone we all know. We should trust no one, the papers say. Is that right, inspector? Is it somebody we know?' she asked deviously.

'I don't think you have anything to fear, Mrs Buller-Price. We're getting there,' he said confidently with equal guile, standing by the old police adage, never to give information away for free.

'I blame alcohol!' she suddenly burst out.

Angel blinked.

'Yes. Alcohol in moderation is a good, social tool, but when taken immoderately is an enemy of the soul. When you get to the bottom of this, inspector, you'll find alcohol is to blame. Only the middle classes should be allowed alcohol. Yes. The lower classes abuse it because it is their only solace, and the upper classes abuse it because the cost is irrelevant to them. Now, inspector, you know that I don't tittle-tattle. I am not a gossip. But about a year ago, for my birthday, with some other groceries and victuals, I ordered a bottle of special Champagne from Heneberry's. Anyway, the following day, I came back from the fields with the dogs, and I found a shipping load of cases and boxes on my doorstep and a bill shoved through the letterbox. It was obviously not my order; for one thing there were four cases of Polish vodka. Four cases! I phoned Heneberry and, of course, they had got the orders muddled. I had got the order intended for Ogmore Hall. In the end it was put right but I couldn't help but wonder. I didn't know Lord Archibald was a drinker! Met him only twice. At NFU do's. He didn't look like a drinker, secret or otherwise. Now I think the vodka may have played a part in his demise. What do you think, inspector?'

The phone rang. Angel looked at it with relief. 'Excuse me,' he said and reached out for it.

It was the superintendent. 'Just had a call from the hospital,' he said urgently. 'An hour ago, in response to an anonymous triple nine, an ambulance picked up a man with gunshot wounds in Jubilee Park. Not carrying any ID. He's in a bad way ... anxious to speak to a policeman.'

Angel breathed out a long sigh. It sounded desperately urgent. 'I'll go straightaway, sir.'

'Ward 12.'

'Right.' The phone went dead.

He looked up at Mrs Buller-Price. 'I have to go. I must apologize. It's an emergency.' Then he stabbed a number into the phone.

Her eyes shone excitedly as she took in the situation. 'That's perfectly all right, inspector. I understand,' she said, quickly reaching down for her stick and bag.

A voice down the phone boomed, 'Transport.'

'DI Angel. This is an emergency. I need a car and driver to take me to the hospital.' 'Right sir. There'll be one at the front in two minutes. It'll have to be a patrol car.'

'Don't care if it's a whippet, if it can carry me and get me there quick!'

He banged down the cradle and dialled another number. He turned to Mrs Buller-Price. 'I'm sorry about this. I'll get Ahmed to show you out.'

'That's all right, inspector. I understand perfectly,' she said, looking alert and interested in the ongoing activity. 'You know, I could drive you there, if you wish?'

'Very kind, but he'll use the siren.' There was a click in the earpiece. 'Cadet Ahaz.'

'Come in here, lad, pronto.'

He replaced the handset and reached out for the crutches.

In less than five minutes he was rocking down the hospital corridor to Ward 12. A woman in a white coat was standing behind a desk at the nurses' base near the door, reading a patient's chart and chewing the end of a pen.

'Excuse me. I'm Inspector Angel from Bromersley Police. I've been called to see a patient ...'

She pointed to an open door behind him with the pen and said, 'In there.'

'How is he?'

She shook her head involuntarily and pursed her lips. Then she abruptly changed. She looked down at the paper she had been reading. 'He's doing *very* well,' she said quickly, then looked back up, nodded and smiled. But it was too late. Her face had given it away. Angel had seen it all before. She smiled with her lips but not with her eyes. His father had died of a gunshot wound in 1987 in this very hospital, and in the same way, he had had to dash there from the station in response to a phone call. He sniffed, squeezed the grips on the crutches, turned, set his jaw and walked through the open ward door.

It was a small, single-bedded room with minimal furniture: bed, locker, sink and chair. In the bed was a patient who had a bandage on his head down to his eyebrows. The only uncovered parts of him were his eyes, nose and mouth. There was a tedious hissing sound of escaping oxygen. A plastic mask hung pointlessly by his chin. The mandatory bleeping machine with a monitor that displayed a moving wavy pattern on a screen and the figure 89, which irregularly changed to 90 and then back again, dominated the other side of the bed. A bag of blood was hanging from a stand with a tube that disappeared under the blankets. A drop of brown liquid dripped into an opaque container fastened to the leg of the bed. Everywhere you looked, there were bags and tubes and wires ...

Angel leaned over the bed and peered closely into the man's pallid, sweaty face. His swollen eyelids were closed, his mouth open. He appeared to be between fifty and sixty years of age and was probably a handsome gadabout in better circumstances.

After a few seconds, Angel sighed, straightened up and moved away from the bedside. He put the crutches across the sink, dragged the chair close to the bed and sat down. Looking across at the bleeping monitor, he rubbed his chin. The bedclothes moved irregularly up and down. There was the whooshing of laboured breathing; the man was fighting for his life.

Quietly, the nurse came in. She was wearing rubber gloves and carrying a loaded hypodermic in a kidney dish. She looked at the patient and then at Angel. 'Still asleep? Has he not woken up? Does he know you're here?'

Angel shook his head. 'No.'

She peeled back the bedclothes, found a suitable place and emptied the syringe. 'He was awake five minutes ago,' she said placing the hypodermic in the kidney bowl and fishing for the pen in her top pocket. She picked up the notes on a clipboard hanging from the bottom of the bed. 'His pulse is down,' she said, sounding pleased. 'I think he'll be awake soon.' Reaching out, she adjusted the oxygen mask over his nose and mouth and went out.

A few moments later, the patient stirred. He rolled his head from one side of the pillow to the other, then he pulled the mask away from his mouth and nose and licked his lips.

Angel stood up and said, 'Hello?'

The man opened his eyes, blinked several times, looked round the room and then peered up at Angel.

He smiled and said, 'I'm DI Angel of Bromersley Police.' He produced a small tape recorder from his coat pocket and switched it on. 'Now what can I do for you?'

'You're a policeman. It's my wife,' he whispered and then winced. 'I think she'll be in great danger.'

'Go on,' Angel said. 'This recorder will catch every word you say.'

He glanced at it and nodded. 'She needs taking away from the house,' he whispered breathily.

'I can do that. But tell me why.'

'It's a long story. Erm ... I stupidly got into debt to a man called Harry Youel ... gambling ... I was never going to be able to pay it back, the interest was getting to be more than the capital ... he knew I was a telephone engineer and he had some racket going ... he offered me a deal to rub out the debt ... three nights' work and I would have paid him off ... I had to agree or I would never have got out of his clutches ... he took me to a big house in the country ... I don't know where it was ... I was blindfolded there and back ... but it must have been north of here ... I felt the sun on my right cheek when I was travelling from there to Bromersley in the late afternoon ... I stayed there ... At nights they drove me back out to connection boxes in and around Bromersley ... I had to fix some circuits to enable him to fiddle the banks. It all went well for him. He made a killing. After three big nights, I thought that was it, and I was out of his clutches ... but no ... he wanted me to fix more lines ... his men, Joshua and Poodle, kept hitting me ... I insisted, I wouldn't do anymore ... anyway, I needed my pills for blood pressure ... he wouldn't let me get them from home ... I became ill ... I had violent headaches ... I couldn't see straight ... I thought

I would die … he threatened me again … I still refused … he said he'd kill my wife! When he saw I was no use to him, he shot me in the stomach … twice I think … I don't know what happened then, I must have passed out.'

'You were picked up in the park, by an ambulance, and brought here.'

'Oh? They must have dumped me there … Anyway, my wife needs taking away from our house immediately, until you get Youel locked up … she doesn't know anything about this … she doesn't know I'm here … will you make sure she's safe?'

'Yes, of course.'

'Promise me.'

'I promise. And I'll tell her where you are. Now what's your name and address?'

'Anton Mulholland. And my wife's name is Adele.'

10

'I want to put that woman in the safe house on Beechfield Walk, sir,' Angel said as he placed a memo on the desk in front of the super.

Superintendent Harker stopped grinding his teeth, picked up the memo and read it. 'Is she a witness?'

'No, but she's the wife of one, and she needs protection while Youel is free.'

He wrinkled his nose, 'Can only shell out board and lodging to witnesses at risk, you know, lad. Not their entourage. This isn't the Holiday Inn!'

Angel's eyes flashed. The skin on the back of his hands tightened. 'I've got a statement from a dying man that will put Youel away for a long time; I promised to see his wife protected until that villain was in custody!'

The super pulled a face like a baby about to cry. 'Can't go making wild promises like that, lad,' he squawked.

'It wasn't a wild promise, sir.'

'Hmmm. It had better be worthwhile. Signed and witnessed is it?'

Angel shook his head. 'It's a recording, sir.'

'A *recording*! And he's *dying*? He'd better live long enough to stand in the box at Youel's trial, if it's going to be worth anything at all. If he dies, your recording isn't worth a stick of liquorice.'

'It's enough to charge him with,' Angel said, his heart pounding.

'You've got to catch him first.'

'Well, I think I know where he is,' he replied, heavily.

The super's little black eyes froze and his bushy ginger eyebrows slid up his forehead. 'Where?'

'At Littlemore school. With his son, Sebastian. It's the only logical place.'

'Don't be daft, lad. Pogle's on obbo there. He would have reported in.'

'Ah well,' Angel said slowly. 'I'm a bit worried about Pogle, sir.'

'What?' he bawled.

'The witness, the man in hospital, Mulholland, said that he was being held by Youel in a big house in the country, north of here. It fits, sir.'

His voice went up an octave. 'Are you suggesting Pogle is letting Youel come and go and shutting a blind eye to it?'

Angel didn't answer, but he looked Harker straight in the eye.

'You're taking a witness's word against a DI's?' the super spluttered.

'There's something else, sir.'

'There'd better be. And you want to be thankful this conversation is off the record,' he said pointing a long blue finger.

Angel's jaw stiffened. 'Oh no sir. I want it putting *on* the record … all I've already said and what I am going to say now.'

The super ground his teeth harder and harder. If he could have breathed out fire, it would have scorched Angel's eyebrows.

'You recall I was ambushed outside the station and offered a bribe by Youel?'

'Yes.'

'I had asked transport to organize a lift to take me home, and I was told I'd be picked up at the front. When I got outside, there was a car already waiting for me. It was one of Youel's cars — not a station car — but I didn't know that at the time. The driver called out my name; he *knew* I wanted a lift.'

'So what? It was coincidence. His man would have been hovering on the off chance. Youel had been wanting to approach you, hadn't he?'

'His man didn't *know* me.'

'He wouldn't *have* to.' He nodded at the crutches on the floor. 'Your Long John Silver outfit would have been a dead giveaway!'

'No sir. No. It was all planned!'

'You're going off your chump, lad. Pogle's got an impeccable record. Served at this station nearly as long as you have. He's as clean as a whistle. His grandfather was mayor of this town. The family's got an impeccable reputation. There's nothing at all to support this daft idea. It's just your creative imagination.'

'No sir. It isn't,' he said firmly.

'Pogle could say the same thing about you, I expect. Haven't you thought how suspicious *your* story was? You said you were ambushed by Youel and two of his men, and taken off in his car. Then you were offered a bribe, which you say you declined. Youel was so delighted, he promptly brought you back here and let you go free and unharmed.'

'I was tipped over the hedge at the front, sir.'

'Huh. A violent crook and his gang, wanted nationally for robbery, robbery with menaces, violence, fraud and a string of other charges, delivered a DI back here to the front door of this police station in broad daylight, in front of those big windows, where he shoved you over a hedge?'

'That's what happened.'

'And you'd not a bruise or a scraped knuckle to show for it!'

'No.'

'You didn't retaliate.'

'I didn't have the chance to retaliate. Look sir. It seems to me it's now or never. Sebastian, we *know*, is there. It's perfectly logical that Harry Youel, his father, would want to be with him. He has to be in the area somewhere. FSU has already been round all the hotels and places offering accommodation. That obbo's gone on long enough. You could say if Harry Youel isn't there now, he's never going to be there.'

The super sighed noisily. 'Trouble with you lad, is that you haven't enough to do. And you've no patience. You've got a nasty multiple murder case in your lap, and just because you're not making any progress with it, you've shifted your attention to this Harry Youel scam.'

Angel was furious. He thought he would explode. He jumped up. His face was burning. 'You brought me into this Harry Youel scam. You wanted me to stand in for Desmond Pogle at that briefing. I didn't volunteer for any of it. Anyway, sir, I hope you have noted my various comments and recommendations. If you don't want me for anything else, I have a lot to do. I'll get on with it.'

The superintendent glared at him, then made a gesture with one hand, the way a   sultan might have used to dismiss a slave.

Angel snatched up the crutches and made for the door, glad to get out of the office. He was so angry: his chest ached. There was a serious risk he might have said something *that* offensive, it might have ended his career.

He stabbed the crutches into the red tiles and made his way purposely up the corridor to his own office. Tossing the crutches into the corner, he dropped into the swivel chair, snatched up the phone and stabbed in a number.

The gentle, polite voice of Cadet Ahmed Ahaz answered. 'Yes sir? Can I help you?'

'Ahmed,' he snapped. 'Get Scrivens to report to me personally, here, now!'

'He'll be at Dr Sinclair's house.'

116

'Then I want to see DS Gawber, here. And I want a printout from the NPC of everything there is on Harry Youel and his associates. The only names I've got for them are a young lad who told me his name was Smith, and two characters that Youel calls Joshua and Poodle. It's urgent, lad. Get your finger out!'

*

'Come in.'

The door slowly opened and DC Scrivens put his head round. 'You wanted to see me, sir?' he asked hesitantly.

Angel looked up from the letter he was reading. 'Come in, lad. Sit down.'

The young man closed the door uncertainly and took the chair by the desk. He pursed his lips and rubbed a hand across his chin.

Angel placed the letter on the pile of papers he was working on and pushed it to the other side of the desk. 'I've got a very important job for you, lad.'

'Oh yes, sir,' Scrivens said, licking his lips.

Angel peered at him. 'Nothing to worry about. You can do this easily. Well, you know Andrew Todd, don't you? He's in DI Pogle's team. Andrew's *about* your age. For reasons that will become clear later, I want you to seek him out and offer to take him for a drink after work tonight.' He reached into his wallet, pulled out a twenty-pound note and handed it to him. 'It's on me, but don't tell *him* that.'

'Oh. Thanks very much, sir,' he said, his jaw dropping open.

'Aye, well hold on. If he says he *can't*, because he's on duty, he might suggest tomorrow night or the night after that. If he does, apologize and tell him you can't because *you* are on duty then, and bring me my money back. Got it?'

'But I'm *not* working tomorrow night, sir, or the night after.'

Angel looked at him closely. 'Things might change, lad,' he said artfully. 'Things might change.'

Scrivens screwed up his eyes as he weighed up the pros and cons of the deal. 'But we *can* go out and spend your twenty tonight, if he's free, sir?'

'Of course, and enjoy yourselves. One more thing ... most important ... as soon as you've found out when he's *off* duty, let me know ... on my mobile. *But don't let him know what you are up to.* Now, push off, find him and set it up, chop chop. And not a word to a soul.'

Scrivens smiled and nodded. He didn't understand the point of it all, but he was enjoying taking part in the subterfuge. 'Right, sir,' he said with a smile and the slightest flicker of one eyelid. Then he went out.

Almost immediately Ahmed came in with a bundle of papers. 'I've got all that the NPC had on Youel and his associates, sir.'

Angel took the file from him with a nod.

There was a knock on the open door and Gawber appeared.

'Come in, Ron.'

He looked very glum. 'I've got some bad news, sir.'

'What?'

'Just had a message from Mrs Mulholland, from the hospital. Her husband died a few minutes ago.'

Angel bit his lower lip and blew out a long sigh, but he soon recovered. It was that sort of news that spurred him on to take big risks.

'Give her my condolences, Ron. They won't help her much, but I don't know what else to say. The best we can do for her and her husband now is to get Harry Youel and his murderous gang put away for a long time.' Gawber nodded.

Angel returned to being very businesslike. 'I want you to take me to the hospital later this afternoon. I've an appointment with the specialist at 1630 hours. Can you do that?'

'Yes sir.'

'Well sit down there a minute,' he said and turned to Ahmed. 'Now lad, I want a double A battery, a strong elastic band, some sticky tape and a lady's hairgrip.'

Ahmed's mouth dropped open.

'Come on, lad. Chop chop.'

Ahmed said, 'Hmm. Yes sir. Now where would I get a battery from?'

'I don't know. Beg one. Steal one. From a clock, a radio. Buy one. I don't care,' he said irritably. 'Just get one. It's very urgent.'

'Well, what do you want it for, sir?'

Angel stared at him. 'I'll tell you that when your voice breaks!' he bawled. 'Now get out and find one, *and* the other stuff. Be quick about it.'

Ahmed didn't reply. He just shook his head and dashed out of the office.

Gawber watched him go and licked his lips. 'Couldn't you be easier on him? He's doing his best.'

Angel's jaw stiffened. He turned round with a face like thunder and stared at Gawber. 'When that lad first came to me, he had to get a note from his mother to cross the road! Now I'm building him up. He's learning that PC doesn't stand for pussy cat. I know, there are plenty of things wrong with me. I am not perfect. But there are plenty of *good* things about me as well. One of them is that I'm not moody. I don't change. I'm as predictable as Syrup of Figs. You can depend on that. *I won't change*. And you want to be glad about that. So don't interfere!'

Gawber was taken aback; he pursed his lips and looked back at Angel. He knew that all he had said was true.

Angel continued, 'So let's get down to it. We've a hell of a lot to do, and not much time to do it in!' He looked at his watch. 'Oh hell! I've got to leave for the hospital in ten minutes!'

*

One of Angel's favourite dishes was finny haddock and brown bread, but Mary noticed he didn't seem very enthusiastic when she put the plate in front of him. He just looked at it, nodded and picked up his knife and fork.

'It's finny haddock,' she said unnecessarily.

'Aye,' he said playing about with a small loose bit that had fallen off the tail as she had been transferring it with the slice from the pan to the plate.

'I thought it was your favourite?' she went on, passing the bread.

After five minutes of silence and very little movement of his knife and fork, she asked, 'What's the matter? Isn't it nice? Mine's delicious.'

'Aye.' He wrinkled his nose and then, tightening his lips, he suddenly said, 'I could kill him!'

Mary looked up in surprise. 'What?' she said. 'Who? Cyril Sagar's dead, Michael. I've been thinking, we ought to go back to Mrs Bailey and see if she can contact your dad and find out what else he might want to say. *That* would settle your mind, I bet.'

Angel frowned. 'I didn't mean *him*. But I'm not wasting fifty quid again to be told a load of nonsense.'

'You didn't 'waste' fifty quid! *I* paid for it. It was third prize I won in the raffle to raise funds in the Mayor's Appeal to restore the Ogmore Fountain. It was a one-pound ticket.'

'Aye, well it *would* cost fifty pounds for two of us to go and have another session.'

'And it wasn't nonsense. It all made sense. She might say something nice, if we went back … about your mother … or your dad.'

'It's a con.'

'You don't know. How do you know?'

She looked at him closely. Intuitively, she said, 'Here Michael, are you making enquiries on the sly?'

He sniffed. 'I might be.'

'I know *you*. That means you *are*. Well you shouldn't be. I think that's awful.'

'Confidence tricksters should be exposed.'

'What have you found out? I bet you find out nothing, and that she's on the up and up. And you shouldn't be doing it, anyway. It's sneaky. It's not right, to be investigating an old woman like that.'

'She's conning people out of hundreds. Some desperately lonely people are spending their pensions on tripe like that!'

'It sometimes gives them a lot of comfort.'

'She didn't say anything derogatory about *your* family.'

'I've been thinking. Have you thought how many interpretations there are of the name Elizabeth?'

'No.'

'Well, there's Elizabeth, Betty, Bet, Bess, Beth, Liza and Liz, to mention a few. And what did your father call your mother? Betty. Now what did Mrs Bailey say your father said? 'Your mother, *Betty*, never stops chinning with your aunt Kate."

'My father didn't have to say 'your mother, Betty.' He *knew* that I knew my mother's name was Betty. He could simply have said, 'your mother'. It *wasn't* him. I've told you!'

'Now you're nit-picking!'

'You're trying to make out a case of honesty that doesn't exist.'

'You'll never be able to prove that your father didn't speak to you through that medium.'

'I probably will be able to show it's unlikely. But *you'll* never be able to prove that he definitely *did*.' Angel put his knife and fork down. 'Mary. Listen to me. It's a con. Somebody feeds information to the old lady. It needs to be somebody who has his or her feet in a place where information about the past is available. If I can prove the existence of a connection between this Selina Bailey and somebody who knew or knew about Cyril Sagar in the 1960s, will you be convinced then?'

'No.'

He shook his head. '*No*??!!' he bawled.

'I'd have to see. It might be coincidence.'

'There's no such thing as coincidence!'

'You're *always* saying that.'

11

It was 08.30 a.m. on Wednesday, 11 May. Four men in dark suits filed into Angel's office wondering why they had been summoned there at such short notice. Ahmed came in last and closed the door.

Angel looked up from his desk and rubbed a hand across his rock-solid chin as he stared up into their sober, enquiring faces. 'Good morning.'

'Good morning, sir,' they replied in unison.

'I know it's a bit crowded; it isn't the briefing room,' he began. 'But relax. There are only two chairs. So, you sergeants take them; you two lads can stand at the side.'

They were soon settled in and Angel began.

'I have called you in here, in secret, to brief you on a rather delicate operation. It is at short notice because it was necessary to time the manoeuvre so that *both* our target villains would be in their respective positions. Last night, Ed Scrivens found out that one of them certainly will be, and I have reason to believe that the *other* will be too. The entire operation should take us about two hours starting from now. Cadet Ahaz will be stationed here, and will be available on his mobile to liaise between us when necessary. We will use only our mobiles. No RT, no land lines. I want you Crisp, and you Scrivens, to work together as a team, and Ron Gawber will work with me. There will just be the five of us. It's a big job for five, but that's how it has to be.'

He went on to specify the targets, he detailed the plan, step by step, and then invited the team to ask questions. There weren't any, so the briefing was over in four minutes. He then established Ahmed in his office, to be private from the rest of the force; Crisp and Scrivens were sent to take up their first position; and he and Gawber set off towards Littlecombe school.

As Gawber drove out of the station car park, Angel began to tell him why he was convinced that Desmond Pogle had taken a bribe from Harry Youel. He went on to say that that was why the force had made no progress in catching the monster and his gang, nor were they ever likely to, now that Pogle was on Youel's payroll. Then he told him about Anton Mulholland's description of the house where he had been accommodated during the few days he had been working for the crook. And he reminded him of his sighting of Youel, Joshua and Poodle as Gawber had been driving him back from Kate Cumberland's the day before. Although he had drawn these facts to the attention of the superintendent, *he* thought they were mere coincidences and he believed that Pogle was dead straight. 'I couldn't say everything in the briefing, Ron. I don't know for certain Youel and his gang are hiding out in the school. We know his son *was* there. But taking everything into consideration, it's the obvious place and the *only* place we have any reason to suspect.'

Gawber nodded and slowed down at the bottom of the hill to go round the Victoria Falls roundabout, then put his foot down, past Ogmore Hall and up the hill.

Angel continued: 'The ATM fiddles have all taken place in the evenings and overnight, so it was reasonable to suppose Youel's gang would be resting up and hiding at the school in the daytime; that's why we're going in now.'

'But DI Pogle will see us arrive from the obbo, won't he?'

'Yes. And by the time they answer the door to me, I expect they will have received a tip-off from him that it is us calling.'

Gawber's mind froze as full realization of the prospect ahead dawned on him. 'But we're not armed! If he tips them off, he'll obviously tell them we are police.'

'Yes.'

'And he *won't* summon the FSU, will he?'

'Almost certainly not,' Angel said significantly. 'And if he doesn't, *then* we'll know for certain he's on the take.'

There was a pause. Then Gawber shook his head. His mouth went as dry as a shroud. 'Well, how are we going to arrest them, if they're armed?'

Angel paused, he wrinkled his nose and said, 'Like we always do, Ron. Like we always do.'

Both men's pulses were banging away as they reached Littlecombe school. Gawber drove the car straight through the open gates, between the stone pillars in the high wall and up the short drive to the front door. He pulled on the brakes and turned off the ignition.

'You stay here,' Angel said as he got out of the car. 'Take it easy. See what happens,' he added in a steady voice.

Gawber nodded and sat motionless, his eyes flitting here and there as he considered the consequences of Youel's gang occupying the school.

'Pass the crutches.'

He passed them through the open window and then frowned. 'I thought you didn't need those anymore?'

'Camouflage,' Angel grunted. He took them and set them under his arms. Then he turned away from the car. The tip of his tongue thoughtfully moistened his lower lip as he glanced up at the pine trees in the copse three hundred yards away. He expected Pogle would be staring back at him through binoculars, while jabbering into his mobile. He took a deep breath and turned towards the stone steps. When he reached the top, he pressed the bell. Fishing in his pocket for his mobile phone, he stabbed in a text message, then held the phone in his pocket with his finger on the 'send' button waiting for the door to be opened. He stood there more than a minute. It seemed longer. His pulse banged in his ears as he imagined the commotion in the house. He rang the bell again, and silently mouthed what he was going to say.

Eventually the door was opened; the very elegant Cynthia Fiske stood there in an expensively cut dark suit, looking as if she had just stepped out of a photo shoot for the Harvey Nichols catalogue. She stared down at him expressionless.

He forced a smile. 'Ah, good morning, Miss Fiske. Michael Angel, do you remember me?'

'Yes. Of course,' she said loftily. 'You're the police inspector,' she added heavily. 'How's your little boy?'

There was no answer to that. He licked his lips. Then he heard the familiar, slow, icy voice. 'I remember you too, Mr Angel.'

It was Harry Youel, but the policeman couldn't see him. He must be concealed behind the door. Eureka! Youel's presence was the confirmation Angel had needed that his hunch had been correct. He pressed the send button on the mobile, then returned his hand to the grip on the crutch.

Cynthia Fiske pulled back the door to reveal three men standing in line: Youel was in the middle, Joshua and Poodle stood towering over him, one on each side.

The scarf no longer covered Youel's face, his open mouth looked like the palette of colours in a children's paint box. He grinned, showing even more colours.

'Do you remember me?' he said breathily.

The hair on the back of Angel's neck stood up. The regular drumming in his ears grew louder.

'Come in. Come in,' the little man said, before Angel could reply.

Pursing his lips, Angel squeezed the grips on the crutches and stepped into the hall.

Cynthia Fiske closed the door.

Youel pointed a finger and the two heavies advanced on Angel like exocets. They pushed his back hard against the door with a bang, and pinned him there by his arms; the crutches clattered noisily to the floor.

Cynthia Fiske glared at Youel, 'Stop them, Harry! Stop them! I've told you before. No rough stuff in *my* house,' she shouted, waving a hand authoritatively.

Youel smiled at her like an undertaker at a centenarian's birthday party. 'Of course, my dear.'

'We don't want any more ... accidents,' she snapped and strode purposefully across the hall to the study.

When the door was closed, Youel turned back to his henchmen. 'Search him. And fetch that other man in and search him too. And move that car out of sight. Quickly!'

Poodle pushed Angel's arms upwards and patted his coat, sleeves and pockets. He found something. It was the mobile. He dug it out of his pocket and handed it to Youel. Then he turned Angel round like a rag doll, pushed his face against the door and patted down his back, buttocks and legs.

'He's clean, Mr Youel,' Poodle said.

Youel pulled a small handgun from his waistband. 'Turn round, Mr Angel, if you please.'

Angel made to turn, bent his right leg under him and collapsed in an untidy heap. He groaned and lay on the highly polished wooden floor for a few seconds. Shuffling round, he straightened out his legs, leaned up and looked at Youel. 'I need my crutches,' he said. But he blinked and froze when he found he was looking down the barrel of a deadly Walther PPK/S automatic. Nobody could miss at a range of six feet.

'You want to be careful where you point that thing. It might go off,' he said angrily.

'Quiet,' Youel said slowly. 'Speak only when you are spoken to,' he added, then turned to the two heavies. 'Move him away from the door.'

Joshua kicked the crutches into a corner, out of their way, then he and Poodle each grabbed a foot and dragged Angel roughly across the polished wooden floor to the centre of the hall.

'Careful!' Angel growled.

'Fetch the other man in, queekly,' Youel said.

They opened the door and ran down the steps.

'And move that car,' he called after them. 'I don't want to advertise we have ... visitors.'

'I need those crutches,' Angel said. 'I want to get up.'

'Quiet. You stay there,' Youel said turning and waving the gun at him.

'I have come to arrest you for the murder of Anton Mulholland,' Angel continued, leaning on his elbows.

Youel looked down at him, flashed the paint box and slowly shook his head. 'I don't think so. In your present position, you couldn't arrest a tortoise.'

There was a rattle as the front door opened. Angel looked round. Joshua and Poodle were frogmarching an ashen-faced Gawber into the hall. The sergeant's arms were up his back causing his eyes to face the floor. The two men propelled him energetically towards the wall and then let go.

Gawber bounced off the wall, turned round, and began to rub life back into his arms. He noticed Angel on the floor. Then, as he straightened up, his jaw dropped when he saw Youel waving the gun.

The front door slammed shut.

Youel looked Gawber up and down. 'Search him.'

The study door was suddenly jerked opened. It was Cynthia Fiske; her eyes were blazing. 'What's that noise?' She saw Gawber. 'Who is this?'

'It's nobody, Cynthia,' Youel said.

She saw the Walther. 'I said, *no guns!*' she shrieked.

The two men pushed Gawber heavily against the door; the letterbox and door chain rattled.

'Is it another policeman?' she said glaring at them. 'I told you, Harry, no rough stuff.'

Youel turned to her. 'Just making it safe for us all, my dear. We have to search him. Won't take a minute.'

Poodle patted down Gawber's arms and pockets.

Joshua looked enquiringly back at Youel.

Cynthia Fiske said, 'I don't want anybody else in here! You understand? This is *not* a hotel!'

Then she noticed Angel on the floor. 'What's this man doing *there*? For goodness sake let him up. Have you lost all sense of propriety?' she yelled.

Angel looked at her. There was so much he would have liked to have said.

Poodle pulled a mobile out of Gawber's pocket and handed it to Joshua, who passed it on to Youel.

Youel looked impatiently across at Cynthia Fiske. 'He's all right where he is, for now. Go away, Cynthia. I know what I am doing. How about making us some breakfast?'

She reached up to her full height, glared at him briefly, then returned to the study and slammed the door.

'He's clean, Mr Youel,' Poodle announced.

'Right. Now, move that car. I'll watch him.'

The two heavies went out through the front door and closed it.

Gawber and Angel exchanged glances. Angel had wanted to smile encouragement to his aide, but the opportunity had now passed. Things were not quite going to plan; his expression reflected the fact.

Youel waved the gun in the direction of the far wall. 'You. What's your name?'

'Detective Sergeant Gawber.'

He made a shaking action with the Walther. 'Sit down Gawber. On the floor. Where you are … that's it.'

There was the sound of light-hearted male voices from upstairs, then running footsteps. Two young men appeared round the turn in the staircase. Angel recognized them both. It was Sebastian Youel with the young man, Smith, who had picked him up outside the station.

As soon as they took in the scene they stopped talking, slowed their step and looked at each other in surprise. 'What's this?' Sebastian said.

'Two bees from the local hive,' Youel answered.

By now the young men had reached the bottom step.

'I know him,' Sebastian said. 'They were both here, last week. He came in pretending he was a parent. The other chap drove him here. I knew there was something fishy about him.'

Youel said, 'Go down and get breakfast going.'

They hesitated.

'Hey,' Sebastian said, turning the corners of his mouth down. 'We ought to get away from here, Dad.'

Youel's left eye twitched. 'Hurry up,' he snarled. 'I'm hungry.'

'What are you going to do with them?'

'Go on. Into the kitchen. Do something useful.'

'Does Mum know?'

His eyes flashed. 'Yes. Yes,' he snapped. 'Get on with it. Both of you. Go.'

The front door opened and Poodle came rushing in. Joshua closed the door and turned the key. 'It's in a garage at the far end, Mr Youel.'

'Right.'

'What do you want us to do with these two?' Poodle said, pointing to the policemen.

'Nothing yet. Get breakfast on. Bring me a coffee and a bacon sandwich.'

Sebastian and Smith passed Youel, went through the door under the stairs and clattered noisily down the wooden steps to the basement, followed by Joshua and Poodle.

Youel stepped a few paces backwards to a big black chair with carved lions forming the arms. He sat down. Curling his lip, he said: 'How did you know I was here?'

'It's our job,' Angel said dryly.

'Who told you? Somebody must have told you. Who else knows I'm here?' Youel shook his head. The question was pointless. Angel wasn't going to say that *nobody* knew they were there, even if it were so.

Angel didn't reply. He caught a glance at Gawber's solemn face. His sergeant was seated on the floor, leaning against the wall near the door. Time ticked away. He checked his watch. It was thirteen minutes since he sent Ahmed the text.

Youel tightened his grip on the gun. 'It doesn't matter what the time is. You're not going anywhere, Mr Angel.'

Angel changed position, lay on his side, and watched Youel, twelve feet away, intermittently flashing the big technicolour teeth when he swallowed as he nervously contemplated his next move.

Angel considered how quickly he could reach his captor's wrist and squeeze the gun free. He could see the safety catch was off, so he would need to be very careful.

Suddenly there was the sound of a raised voice downstairs.

'What? What have you done with them? I've got to have them!' Then there was the sound of crashing furniture, followed by a yell before another voice spoke out.

Harry Youel's nostrils flared and he bared his teeth as he glanced towards the basement doorway.

It had sounded like Sebastian.

The study door opened and Cynthia Fiske dashed out.

'Now what's happening?' she shouted.

Youel nodded towards the basement door and scowled.

'Sebastian and Smithy, I think. Will you go down and shut them up?'

There were more raised voices coming from the basement now.

She ran across the hall and through the door, her high heels clattering noisily down the steps. There were exchanges between Sebastian and Cynthia, then another voice joined in the ruckus.

Angel and Youel strained to hear what was happening.

Two minutes later, Sebastian came rushing up the steps, followed by Smith. Cynthia Fiske clattered up after them. All three came through the doorway in quick succession.

Sebastian rushed up to Youel and yelled, 'Smithy's taken my dazzies!'

Youel stood up, glanced quickly at Sebastian, then stared hard back at Angel and then at Gawber.

Cynthia sighed and said, in a bored voice, 'He says Smithy has taken his pills.'

The young man said, 'I've never touched his pills. I don't do dazzies. I've got my own stuff.'

'He *must* have,' Sebastian yelled.

Youel snarled, shook his head angrily and said, 'What pills? What you talking about?'

'My dazzies. The whole boxful. I haven't any left!'

Youel looked at Cynthia.

She pulled an impatient face. 'He means diazepam,' she said slowly, translating. Then she added, furiously, 'I know nothing about it. But I do know that, between them, they've broken the hinge on the cupboard door and chipped the Royal Doulton milk jug.' She put her hands in the air in exasperation and beat a path for the stairs.

'I'll get you a new kitchen … in a palace,' Youel called after her.

'*No thank you,*' she shouted back, with heavy emphasis on each word.

'It was an accident,' Sebastian called.

She continued down the steps.

Smith said, 'It was Sebastian, Mr Youel. He was going through my pockets.'

'You must have taken them when I was asleep.'

Youel shook his head irritably. 'We can get some later.'

'I need them now!' Sebastian wailed.

Youel said, 'Can you give him some?'

Smith sniffed and shuffled his shoulders like a boxer before a bout. 'I can *sell* him some, I s'pose,' he said pertly, standing with his back towards the basement steps.

Youel's face went scarlet. He breathed in noisily through his nose. His eyes went the colour of burning cinders. '*Sell* him some?' he snarled. 'You ungrateful little —'

He leaped over to the young man and pushed him viciously on the chest with the gun. Smith staggered backwards, through the open basement door. He yelled and fell away into nothingness, his arms reaching pointlessly up in the air.

Youel turned back to see Angel already on one knee, and Gawber standing. 'Get down. Get down!!' he shrieked, waving the gun at them.

They had to retreat.

Smith screamed as his body bounced six times down the bare wooden basement steps. The banging was followed by the sound of splintering wood, then there was an ominous silence.

Sebastian's face went white. He looked at his father, his mouth open wide.

Harry Youel shrugged, then grinned. He backed off from the basement door and returned to the chair.

Sebastian went rushing down the steps. 'Smithy. Smithy.'

It stayed quiet downstairs.

Angel rubbed his chin as he strained to hear any sound that would indicate the condition of the young man. The quieter it was, he thought, the more serious the outcome might be. It was very quiet indeed. The cavalier attitude displayed by Youel did not augur well for his and Gawber's safety.

Five minutes later, Poodle came slowly up the steps with a mug of coffee in one hand and a plate with a bacon sandwich in the other. He handed them to Youel, who flashed all thirty-two colours and stuffed the Walther in his waist band. Putting the coffee on the floor, he got stuck in to the sandwich.

Poodle ambled off back down the stairs.

Angel looked at his watch; it was now twenty minutes since he had signalled Ahmed. Youel noticed the movement. He continued chewing for a few seconds, then said, 'You've come off your own bat, haven't you? The brains department wouldn't send a man on crutches to take me on, would they?' he sniggered and took another bite at the sandwich. 'You must be mad. Did you think you could intimidate me and then take me back with you like a puppy dog on a string? Because if you did, you are stupid.'

132

Angel sniffed. 'Somebody has got to do it. And you are wanted for murder and a string of other offences.'

'No, Mr Angel. Not guilty of murder. Not guilty of anything.' The corners of his huge mouth turned up, simulating a smile, but his eyes remained half-closed.

Angel looked at him briefly and wrinkled his nose. He was a very ugly man. He had the sort of head you find skewered on a door in Africa.

Youel bit off another chunk of the sandwich and continued chewing. Suddenly he seemed to have had an idea. Reaching into his pocket, he pulled out his mobile and tapped in a number. The number rang out for a few seconds. As soon as it was answered, he stopped chewing. His face changed. He jumped up. His lips curled cruelly. 'Who is that?' he snarled, gripping the phone tightly. 'I want to speak to Pogle ... Who is that? *Who?* ...' His eyes opened wide briefly; they nearly popped out of his head. His hand was shaking. He suddenly glared down at Angel. '*What?*' he screamed. '*What?*'

Angel smiled. His pulse rate doubled and his face flushed up. He guessed his cheeks must be scarlet.

Youel threw the mobile wildly across the room at him; it missed by miles, hit a radiator, chipped the silver paint and rattled noisily on the parquet floor.

There was the clatter of high heels up the basement steps. Cynthia Fiske appeared in the doorway. She was panting. Her face was white and she had a hand to her temple.

He turned to face her. 'This place has been rumbled,' he screamed, his left eye twitching. 'The lookout has gone. I've got to get out of here. Tell the boys. We're leaving, now!'

Angel's heart sank; they mustn't get away.

'Smithy needs a doctor. He'll have to go to hospital,' she said urgently.

'It was nothing, Cynthia. I dropped my phone. That is all. It is nothing,' he said as if she'd not uttered a word.

'I must ring the hospital,' she said.

'No,' he yelled.

'I must. You're not taking Sebastian?' she said anxiously.

'Tell him to get packed *fast*, Cynthia. He's got to come. He hasn't any transport.'

'You could get him a car.'

'There's no time. He can't drive. Anyway, if he's found here, he'll be arrested. Tell him to get a move on.'

'He's not going with you.'

'It's up to him. Are you coming with me?' She raised her elegant head, looked down at him and said, 'Don't be ridiculous!'

'Don't say I didn't give you the chance. We could start all over again.'

She snorted, lifted her nose, turned and ran down the steps. Seconds later she came back. Her eyes were staring, her face pale. 'Smithy is in a bad way. He really needs a doctor.'

'He'll be all right. We'll leave him here. There's no time!'

'He needs medical attention *now*. His head is bleeding. He needs a doctor, or he'll die!'

'We're going. Where are they?' he yelled. 'And get me some rope. A clothes line.'

'What for? I'm ringing for an ambulance.'

'No. Not yet. We are leaving *now*. You can ring when we've gone,' he screamed.

Youel went over to the basement door and called, 'Joshua! Poodle! Sebastian! All of you. Come up here.'

'Aren't you even going to look at him?' she said, her eyes shining.

'I'm not a doctor. I can't help him. I must get away. Get me a clothes line.'

Youel stared at Angel. He was about to say something when there was a loud clattering on the basement steps. He turned to look.

Joshua and Poodle came in.

Cynthia turned and went back down the steps.

Youel sighed. 'Where's Sebastian?'

They didn't reply. They looked at each other and then shrugged. Neither wanted to incur his wrath by telling him what they knew.

Youel glanced at Angel and Gawber and said, 'Watch them. Don't take your eyes off them. We're leaving. Now.' He handed the Walther to Poodle.

The lump nodded and took the gun.

'Joshua, bring my car round to the front. And get the small car out; Poodle will drive that. We'll be out in a couple of minutes,' he said quickly.

'Right, Mr Youel. What about them?' Joshua pointed towards Angel and Gawber.

'I'll see to them!' he shrieked impatiently. 'Now get on with it!'

Poodle's jaw dropped open. Joshua's eyebrows shot up. They exchanged glances. They were used to Youel's moods, but this was probably unusually extreme.

Joshua crossed rapidly to the front door and ran out.

Youel turned and ran down the basement steps. 'Cynthia! Sebastian!'

Angel meanwhile took the opportunity to make six inches towards Poodle and the gun.

The mountain saw him. 'Keep still,' he growled and stared at each of his prisoners in turn. He backed up slowly to the big chair and eased himself into it.

Angel stared up at the bruiser. He sighed as he wondered whether he and Gawber were going to get out of this situation alive. Suddenly, he heard raised voices from the basement. There seemed to be a heated argument between Sebastian, his father and Cynthia Fiske. It didn't last long. Light feet clattered rapidly up the basement steps. Poodle heard them and stood up. It was Harry Youel wearing a raincoat, hat and scarf, and carrying a clothes line and a briefcase. He glanced quickly at Angel, Gawber and then Poodle; he dropped the briefcase where he stood and dropped the clothes line over the newel post.

'Tie him to the chair, quickly,' Youel snapped. 'Stand up, Angel.'

'I'll need my crutches,' he said and pointed to them lying on the floor in the far corner. He slowly got to his knees and made to sit up.

Youel wrinkled his nose and said, sneeringly, 'There's no time.' He dashed across the room to him. 'Stand up. Stand up!' he bawled impatiently and put his hands out to grab Angel's shoulders and yank him up to his feet. Momentarily, he was between the Walther and Angel, and Angel knew it! It was long enough. The inspector shot to his feet like a champagne cork, grabbed the little man with one hand and swung him round to face Poodle. With his arm round Youel's neck, he stuck the double A battery he had been secreting in his sweaty hand for the last ten minutes, hard into the man's spine and pulled him back on to it.

'*Put your hands up and don't move*,' Angel said in the most Cagney-like manner he could manage. '*My* time has come,' he added menacingly.

Youel froze.

Poodle gripped the Walther hard. His hand was shaking. His eyes flashed as he glanced first at Gawber then at Angel.

'Put your hands up! *Now!*' Angel repeated.

Youel's hands flew upwards. 'I thought you had searched him, you imbecile!'

'I did, Mr Youel. He *can't* have a gun,' Poodle whined.

Angel felt his pulse drum in his ears. His face went white. 'You should have been more thorough,' he snapped.

Gawber slowly stood up and looked across at Angel. He wondered just how bold he could be.

Poodle's hand was shaking. He turned from Gawber to Youel, his face a picture of confusion.

'Don't point that thing this way, you fool!' Youel bawled. 'Point it at him!' he added nodding towards Gawber.

Gawber put up his hands, but remained standing.

Through clenched teeth, Angel said to Youel: 'We are going to move back to the wall. If you *don't* want to live in a wheelchair for the rest of your life, you'll come straight backwards with me, now.' The two men edged back together until Angel felt the ridges of the radiator press on his legs. He stopped, released the grip round Youel's neck, but kept the battery pressed firmly into his back.

Poodle stared hard ahead at Gawber, his gun hand still shaking. A shiny surface of perspiration glistened on the big man's forehead. 'What do you want me to do, Mr Youel?'

'Nothing,' he said evenly, then he looked towards Gawber and added, 'Shoot him if he moves.'

Again Angel pushed the battery into the little man's spine.

Youel screamed. 'No. Don't do *anything*! Don't do anything, until I tell you. Have you got that, Poodle? Don't do anything.'

'Right, Mr Youel,' he said, licking his fat lips.

There was a natural pause.

Angel wondered where he was going from there. Any second now, Joshua was going to come in through the front door looking for Youel, and Sebastian or Cynthia might come up stairs to see what was happening. Either intrusion, if mishandled, could end in his death and Ron Gawber's. It was a Mexican stand-off that depended entirely on bluff, but he could not maintain the bluff forever, and Joshua might just be the one thick enough to call it!

The front door suddenly opened. It was Joshua. Without looking round the hall, he turned, pushed the door almost shut and then, hanging on to the knob, peeped back outside through the gap. 'We've no transport, Mr Youel,' he yelled frantically. 'All four tyres in both cars *and* the police car are flat. They've had the valves taken out. There's somebody out there. Must be. Can't see them. Can't *see* anybody. What are we going to do?' He banged the door shut, turned the key and looked round. His jaw dropped when he took in the scene.

'Stay where you are,' Angel said commandingly. 'Put your hands up.'

Joshua took a step forward.

Angel jabbed at the battery.

'Stay there, Joshua,' Youel screamed. 'Stay there. He's got a gun in my back. Do as he says.'

Joshua stopped instantly. He stood there, his feet apart. He looked at Youel and Angel, then at Poodle and the Walther, and then at Gawber with his hands up, then back at Youel and Angel. He raised his hands slowly. 'He didn't have a gun when he was searched, Mr Youel,' he said evenly.

Angel felt his heart flutter. His collar was tightening round his neck. 'Is he calling me a liar?' he heard himself call out.

Youel quickly said, 'No. No. You're not, are you, Joshua? You're not calling Mr Angel a liar?'

'No. No,' Joshua said uncertainly. 'No.' His mouth dropped open, he looked across at the bizarre sight of Angel rammed up close behind Youel and frowned.

Angel tried to look more dangerous. He had to make the bluff last as long as possible. He reckoned if he was exposed, Joshua was strong enough to take Gawber and himself on and squeeze them both to death with one hug. He didn't want to get in a tangle with *him*. He glanced at his watch. It was over thirty-two minutes since he had sent Ahmed the text message. He hoped nothing had gone wrong. He tried to swallow. His mouth was as dry as a shroud. Sebastian and his mother wouldn't stay downstairs with the injured Smithy forever … if they came upstairs …

Suddenly, there was a loud knock on the front door. 'Open up. It's the police!'

Youel noisily sucked in a bucketful of air: Angel blew out a barrel's worth.

It was the FSU: better late than never!

Joshua's head swivelled round to the door. The whites of his eyes caught the light as he checked everybody's face in quick succession. Poodle renewed his tight grip on the Walther and licked his lips. Gawber stood helpless, facing him, hands still in the air.

The door knob rattled. Loud banging followed. 'Open up! It's the police.'

'You'd better unlock the door and open it, Joshua,' Angel said evenly.

The big man looked at Angel, then at Youel. But he didn't move and stayed frozen to the spot.

Angel jabbed the battery into Youel's spine; the little man gasped but didn't speak. Angel's heart began to thump. He could hear drumming in his ears. He jabbed the battery harder.

Youel responded. 'Open the door, Joshua. For god's sake!' he squealed.

Joshua shook his head slightly but didn't move anything else.

Poodle stared straight ahead at Gawber; he gripped the Walther so tight his hand was shaking like butterfly wings. Gawber stood there licking his lips with his hands up and praying for a miracle.

The noise at the door grew louder. 'Police. Come on! Open up!'

Angel jabbed the battery fiercely into Youel's back again and said, 'You'd better get him to open the door if you don't want hot lead in your colon!'

Youel couldn't hold out any longer. 'Open the door, Joshua! Open the door!' he shrieked.

'He hasn't a gun, Mr Youel,' Joshua yelled, lowering his hands. 'He can't have. He's bluffing.'

Youel began to shake.

Poodle said, 'What do you want me to do, Mr Youel?'

He didn't reply.

Joshua said, 'I'm not going back inside for nobody!'

Angel pressed the battery hard into the little man's back again and shouted, 'Get him to open that door, or prepare yourself for a one-way trip in a hearse!'

'Open the door, Joshua,' Youel wailed. 'Open the door!'

The man didn't move. He just stood there, his eyes glazed. He started to flap his hands by his sides, glancing alternately at the door and then at Angel.

Angel's brain raced. He was worried about Gawber. He was directly in the line of fire.

The police were still clamouring at the heavy door.

'Shall I let him have it, boss?' Poodle said, staring at Gawber, his hand shaking.

'If you do, *he* gets it,' Angel bawled. 'Open that door now, Joshua, or this man *never* walks again!'

Angel heard footsteps and voices on his right coming up from the basement. The arrival on the scene of Sebastian Youel and Cynthia Fiske now would be disastrous.

Angel was desperate … out of ideas, out of fighting talk and losing credibility faster than a PM in his third term. Joshua was about to call his bluff and escape. Poodle would certainly pull the trigger on Gawber if he did.

Suddenly, through the open basement door, five men clad in navy blue and black uniforms, wearing helmets with 'Police' marked on them and brandishing Heckler and Koch carbines piled in. They yelled, 'Police. Police. Stay where you are. Get down on the floor. On the floor. On the floor. *Down*! *Down*!! *Down*!!!'

Angel sighed with relief as he saw DI Waldo White dash boldly over to Poodle and relieve him of the Walther.

One of the policemen opened the front door and two more FSU men rushed in. There was the rattle of handcuffs and the swishing sound of webbing against satin-covered body armour.

Angel relaxed his grip on Youel, who lowered his arms and gasped. A policeman jabbed him in the arm with a Glock 17. He glowered, bent his knees and crawled to the floor.

Angel sighed with relief. He was desperately anxious to reach Ron Gawber and looked across the sea of helmets, uniforms and guns.

Then, amidst all the yelling, rattle of rifles and jingle of handcuffs he heard his name being called, 'Mr Angel. Mr Angel.' It came from a voice at his feet.

He looked down at the toothy horror and shook his head in disgust. What a boon to the boatmen of the Zambesi Youel would be, frightening the crocodiles.

'We can still do a deal, Mr Angel,' he said looking up with froglike eyes. 'It's not too late. You can get me out of this. Make it fifty thousand!'

'No thank you,' he sniffed and waved his hand. Then he realized he was still holding the double A battery. 'But I'll leave you with his,' he said quietly and, opening his sweaty hand, he let the battery drop to the floor by Youel's head. 'You might need it, for your calculator,' he said, with a nod, 'to add up the number of years you're going down for.'

12

'Come in lad. Shut the door.'

'Did it go all right, sir?'

Angel pursed his lips. 'It was a close call. FSU were late.'

'I phoned them just as you instructed sir. They got lost.'

'*Lost*! Some folks'd get lost in their own bathroom! How did the super take it?'

'He was furious,' Ahmed said evenly.

Angel smiled.

There was a knock at the door.

'Come in.'

It was DS Crisp.

Angel looked up. 'Come in, lad. Come in. Did Pogle give you any trouble?'

He shrugged. 'It was a bit awkward arresting a DI. But when I'd got the cuffs on him, and he understood that we meant business, he calmed down.'

Angel nodded.

Crisp pulled a small polythene bag out of his pocket. 'What shall I do with these, sir?'

'What are they?'

'Valves from the car tyres.'

Angel smiled. 'I told you it would be easy. Give them to Ron. Some of them are from his car.'

Crisp grinned. 'Never thought you could do it with a hairgrip.'

The inspector smiled. When the phone rang, he reached out for it. 'Angel.'

It was superintendent Harker.

The smile vanished.

'Ah, you're back,' he growled. 'Bring yourself down here.'

Angel pulled a face. 'Right, sir,' he said and replaced the phone. He pursed his lips and sighed. He knew he had to take his medicine sometime, so he was down the green corridor straightaway. He tapped on the door.

'Come in,' the superintendent bawled. Looking up at him, he frowned. 'Sit down.' Then his eyebrows shot up. 'Where are your crutches?'

'They took the plaster off yesterday, sir.'

'Oh?' he sniffed uncertainly. 'You can walk all right now then, can you?'

'Yes sir.'

'Hmmm. So you didn't actually need crutches this morning, then?'

'No, sir.'

'Hmmm.' The superintendent sniffed and slowly reached forward on the desk and opened a thin cream file. He appeared to read a few sentences before looking up. His face had changed from basic ugly to advanced repulsive. He took in a deep breath, looked Angel in the eye and said, 'What's the idea of going off half-cock on a job, unarmed and unbriefed, to capture a dangerous hoodlum like Youel? Who the bloody hell do you think you are, James Bond?'

Angel's mouth dropped open. He was not really surprised at the superintendent's outburst. Knowing him well enough, he also knew he couldn't be in that much trouble because he had Youel and his gang — and Pogle — in custody and there weren't any casualties.

'Haven't I the authority to mount an assault, when I have good reason to believe I know where a wanted criminal is in hiding?'

Harker stuck out his lips like a pig sticks out its snout. 'I'm saying there wasn't any proper coordination *and* cooperation in the planning. I didn't know anything about it, for one. And you deliberately blew Pogle's obbo without consulting me. If you had been wrong about him, you would have made a right mess of things.'

'You didn't want to hear anything wrong about Desmond Pogle, sir. I sounded you out on that specifically. You wouldn't have given me your cooperation to set up a trap to —'

'I wasn't in possession of all the facts then, man!' he bawled. 'That's why I wouldn't go down that path!' He began grinding his teeth. 'And you admit you deliberately went behind my back because you didn't get my agreement to this unsupported idea?'

'No. Not at all. I told you *all* I knew. And it was necessary to *contain* that intelligence. The operation was carried out by me and four men only at very short notice, because I couldn't risk Youel bunking off, or Pogle getting wind of it in the canteen or somewhere. And, it was a golden opportunity to catch two birds with one stone. There wasn't much time. It was a cheap, quick, small, successful operation, without any casualties. We winkled out a bent copper and got Harry Youel and his gang off the streets inside two hours.'

The super wrinkled his nose. He didn't want to agree, but he was having difficulty finding anything more to gripe about. Yet, he continued. 'A man's in hospital in a serious condition,' he added, pretending that he cared.

'That was nothing directly to do with the operation. It was a family row over drugs.'

He sniffed, then nodded slowly. 'You were *very* lucky. *Very* lucky! There were a million things that could have gone wrong. You'd absolutely no back-up, and I wouldn't have been able to support you if anything *had* gone wrong.'

Angel knew *that* was true and it was typical that now, knowing that everything had gone *right*, he *still* didn't choose to support him!

'Yes sir,' he agreed, to try to draw the subject to a close.

The super cleared his throat noisily and said, 'Aye. Right. Well, let's get down to the nitty gritty. Pogle has been charged, I've seen to *that*. We had to have something to hold him on, but of course there's a lot more than disciplinary charges involved here. It will have to go to the divisional commissioner.' He turned the corners of his mouth down. 'I want Pogle moved out of this station *today*. He can go to Doncaster after he's been to court, or anywhere, the further the better. I want him out of my sight. I never could *stand* the man. I always thought there was something not quite above-board about him. It was a good job we caught him when we did. You know, he came from a very unsavoury family. His grandfather was always on the take when he was mayor,' he said, wrinkling his nose and shaking his head.

Angel blinked in astonishment but didn't say anything.

'Get Todd to clear his office and stuff,' he said pursing his lips. He reached out for his pen and looked down at the file. 'Right. Now, have we anything on this Fiske woman?' he asked rubbing his chin. He looked up. 'Is she his wife or his fancy woman or what?'

'They're divorced, sir. She's his ex-wife and mother of Sebastian.'

'Oh.' The superintendent shook his head. 'He's an ugly man,' he said pulling a face like a tray of tripe.

Angel stifled a smile. 'Yes, sir.'

'Can't see what she saw in him,' he muttered. 'Is there anything to charge her with? Harbouring? Aiding or abetting? Or —'

'I don't think we'd make anything stick. She clearly didn't want her ex-husband and his gang there. He was simply taking advantage of their past relationship and the fact that *their* son, Sebastian, was visiting her.'

The superintendent frowned. 'Hmmm. How on earth did Youel manage to bag a well-set-up woman like Cynthia Fiske? I mean, she's not bad-looking, well educated and she's obviously got a bob or two? *And* taller than him as well.'

'The stuff on the NPC said she was university-educated, a teacher, good family. Did voluntary work … a prison visitor, and she met Harry Youel while on her rounds at Brixton in the eighties … eventually married him in '83, she helped him get on his feet on his release … no doubt thought she could civilize him and has probably regretted it ever since. Of course, they had a baby … just the one. But he was always in jail for robbery as a young man, lately much bigger jobs and thuggery. She divorced him in 1988 and reverted to her maiden name. Then she bought the school in Littlecombe well away from London, after her parents died. It would be because of Sebastian, I suppose, that Youel eventually traced her there.'

'Some women are just plain stupid,' Harker said grinding his teeth. 'They panic like hell when they reach thirty-five and they haven't had a baby. Anyway, I'll have a word with the CPS, see if there is anything. Now what about the lad, Sebastian?'

'Nothing new on him, sir. Might get him on possession of Class C. Difficult to prove. His father going down might be enough to scare him off? I reckon his mother, given half a chance, could straighten him out.'

The superintendent looked down at the notes in the file. 'Hmmm. And the lad that's in hospital. What's his name? Smith?'

Angel frowned. 'Possession of Class C. Again, it would be hard to prove. Might be something in his past. Nothing else known.'

'Really? Right. That's it, then,' the superintendent said as he threw his pen down.

They both sighed.

Angel thought Harker was pleased. He should be, but he'd never say it.

'What's going to happen now, sir? There's a lot of paper-work to see to, sorting out the charges with the CPS, and follow through, and tidy up. Pogle can't do it. Are *you* going to finish it off, sir?'

'Oh no, lad. You're the one that knows most about it,' he said, handing him the file.

*

'Ahmed, I asked you to get me a list of the phone calls made by that charlatan, Selina Bailey, for the past month …'

'It's on your desk, sir. There. Somewhere.'

'Where?' Angel barked impatiently. He shuffled through the pile of envelopes and papers that had come in that day. 'Aye. It's here.'

'I've had a look at it, sir,' Ahmed said pointing at the paper. 'It's not a long list. I've written in, in pencil, *where* she rang. She doesn't seem to phone anyone who *isn't* in business. I don't think there are any calls to family or friends. I didn't think you'd be interested in local calls to shops, an optician, the chemist's. And the only non-local she made was to Leeds … to a chemical company … Schofields Yorkshire Chemicals. Now, she rang them each Thursday morning. Can't think what she'd want with them.'

'No lad. I can't either,' he said. He reached over for the phone and dialled a number.

It was answered by a young lady with a squeaky voice: 'Schofield's Yorkshire Chemicals. Charlotte speaking. How can I help you?'

'Ah yes. I'm calling on behalf of Mrs Bailey, 28 Huddersfield Road, Bromersley.'

'Oh yes? Did she want to place an order?'

'Well, she asked me to query last Thursday morning's call,' he said. He pursed his lips and listened hopefully.

'Oh yes? What exactly is the problem? The order was delivered all right on Friday, wasn't it?'

'I think so. That's not exactly what she asked me to phone about,' he said and then he shut up, just held the handset and looked up at the ceiling.

'Let me have a look at what she has on order ... Mmmm ... Now, she usually has a ten-kilo block of Cardox, doesn't she? Delivered on a Friday.'

'I think so,' he said nodding happily. 'Ah well, she was wanting to know what exactly is in it?'

'Oh? Well I am sure it will be suitable for what she needs it for. It's pure, deep-frozen one hundred per cent carbon dioxide. That's all it is.'

'Ah,' Angel said, his face brightening. 'Right. Thank you.'

'Did she want any on Friday?'

'I expect she'll phone you tomorrow as usual. Thank you very much, Charlotte. Goodbye.'

He replaced the phone.

Ahmed looked at him expectantly. 'Did you find out, sir?'

'Aye,' he said with a smile. 'She buys Cardox, frozen carbon dioxide, from them.'

Ahmed looked blank. 'What's that, sir?'

'It's for refrigeration, keeping things cold. Looks like ice, but it leaves nothing behind, no water. As it melts or thaws, it turns into gas and disperses into the air. It is sometimes used by funeral directors, hospitals, ice-cream vendors and TV and film set designers. It comes in a block, and it's usually delivered in an insulated container. In this instance,' he said slowly and with a big smile, 'it explains cold feet and the remains of a spirit disappearing in a cloud of mist in the drawing room of Selina Bailey's front room on Huddersfield Road!'

The young man's mouth dropped open.

There was a knock at the door.

'Come in.'

It was Gawber. 'I'm just back from the bank, sir. Saw the assistant manager. Geoffrey Sanson wasn't one of their favourite customers. He was always exceeding his overdraft limit. They occasionally had to stop his cheques.'

'Oh?' Angel pursed his lips. 'Hmmm. That's how it was, eh?' He turned to Ahmed. 'Did you find that chap, Benny Peters?'

'Yes sir. He is a bookie, sir. Got a shop in Temptation Yard. Opposite the Town Hall. Nothing known.'

'Do you want *me* to call on him, sir?' Gawber asked.

Angel looked up from the desk. 'No. Finish off at Sinclair's ... and if you see any freshly turned earth on your travels ...'

Gawber frowned and turned back.

Angel wrinkled his nose. 'The murderer's clothes would have some blood on them. Probably quite a lot. Would need somewhere to bury them or burn them ...'

'Ah yes,' he said thoughtfully. 'Right sir. I'll keep my eyes open.'

Angel watched Gawber go out and close the door behind him. He rubbed his hand across his chin a few times, then turned to Ahmed.

'Yes sir?' he replied brightly.

'What do you know about Polish vodka?'

'Polish vodka? It's an alcoholic drink, sir, isn't it? Looks like water. Doesn't smell on your breath.'

'Precisely. Hmm. So presumably anybody could sup the stuff and no one would be any the wiser ... unless they're falling about the place ... or slurring their words ...'

Ahmed stared at him and wondered what he was getting at, but said nothing.

Angel pulled the pile of papers and post that had increased over the past two days towards him. He sniffed and said, 'I've got more paperwork than Carol Vorderman's manager. Go on, lad. Hop off. I've a lot to do.'

Suddenly the door opened. 'Can I come in?' It was Mac.

Angel looked across. 'Aye,' he said smiling.

As Mac came in, Ahmed went out.

'I've got a present for you,' he said in that Glaswegian dialect singularly his around Bromersley station.

Angel nodded. 'Sit down.'

Mac slid into the chair, opened a brown envelope and gently tipped the contents over the desk. Two dangerous-looking stilettos clattered out.

Angel wrinkled his nose and reached out for them. 'Ah,' he said and nodded. 'The same as the other two.'

'Two more to go to make the half-dozen,' Mac said ominously.

Angel sniffed. 'Any prints?'

'No. Just gloves.'

'Anything else? Footprints? DNA?' he asked eagerly. There was a pause. 'Anything?' he added hopefully.

'Nope. Nothing,' Mac said, rubbing his chin. 'The murders would be silent, bloody and quick. Same as the others.'

Angel shook his head and blew out a long sigh. 'What I particularly don't like, is that the murderer is obviously someone we know, probably brushing up against, perhaps on a daily basis, or even several times a day. No wonder there's a sort of nervousness around the town. It's somebody we know, somebody you might work with, see at an auction, stand next to in a shop, or have knock on your door to return something they borrowed.'

'Aye. My wife's got the heebie-jeebies,' Mac said grimly. 'Her friends in the butcher's and the hairdresser's are the same. Won't open the door if I'm not there. Day or night. And I can't get out to the pub now. She won't be left on her own.'

'Mary's the same.'

'I thought you had a lead on that couple of lumps with ponytails.'

'They keep popping up. I got a witness who *almost* saw them thump Geoffrey Sanson outside the auction house. Since then, they've disappeared. Whoever they are, whatever they are, they're harder to get hold of than an apology from the prime minister. Which reminds me, could vodka be responsible for the condition of Geoffrey Sanson's liver, *Polish* vodka?'

'Of course. Sounds a very possible candidate, Michael. Have you got some evidence that that was his tipple?'

'No. Not evidence. Information from a witness, in passing, you might say.'

'Any alcohol taken regularly in excess will turn your liver to yellow Wensleydale in no time.'

'Mmmm. Well, those two men … if it is those two men, what are they looking for? Money? Deeds? There wasn't any cash in the houses. Or drugs. And Lady Ogmore's bungalow had a lot of small, portable treasures, but nothing was taken. Whatever it is, they haven't found it yet or they would have stopped looking and stopped killing.'

'Can't help you there, Michael.'

Angel sighed. 'It *shouldn't* be as difficult as this, Mac. Look at how much blood was spilled at each murder scene. That's a fair amount of clothing stained … ruined — coat, shirts, ties, dresses, skirts.'

'And gloves.'

'Aye, and gloves. Whoever it is, at least three sets of clothes would have had to be burned or buried somewhere. Is that one fire, or three fires? There are very few open coal fires where you could quickly dispose of a suit and a shirt and a pair of gloves. Or is it one hole in the ground or three holes? We are dealing with a very efficient murdering machine; it's hardly likely such damning evidence is being saved and stored in a wardrobe, under a bed or in the boot of a car! By the way, *you* haven't seen any newly turned earth in your travels, have you?'

'No.' Mac's eyes narrowed. He looked closely at Angel and said, 'Can I put another aspect to you, Michael? Have you considered that sticking a stiletto in somebody with the certainty you are terminating a life requires a person of a particular temperament? Once the tip of that blade pierces the skin, the victim will be effectively dead in two seconds. No ifs and buts. It's not like firing off a gun in response to something that frightens you. The victim might survive and give evidence; also you could be yards away from him. Applying a stiletto necessitates some emotional preplanning; it requires you to be actually close up to your victim. For that last second, at the very least, he can see you and you can see him, and *he* will know you are killing him!'

Angel nodded. 'You know Mac, I think the murderer or murderers must be hyped up with something. Something powerful. Like a needle full of cocaine?'

'Aye. Half a bottle of whisky would do it.'

'Or vodka?'

'Or vodka. Yes.'

'Trouble is, I can't find a suspect who regularly sups vodka, sticks needles in or —'

'You won't,' Mac interrupted, his eyes stared unblinking across the desk. 'They'd do it on the sly.'

Angel nodded. 'And it's somebody associated with, or very close to, the Ogmores. I reckon Mrs Sinclair was the exception. She got in the way and had to be killed to allow the murderer to search the house. After all, her husband was the doctor who attended the Ogmores.'

'All roads lead back to Ogmore Hall. The butler, the housekeeper and the doctor who were murdered ... and that secretary, Kate Cumberland, and Lady Emerald herself, whose places were turned over but both live to tell the tale ...'

'Aye and if the murderer can't find whatever he's looking for, he'll be back. It might be staring him in the face and he can't see it. Do you think Lady Emerald is safe? Kate Cumberland has a husband or a partner or, well, she lives in with somebody. Lady Emerald is on her own. Now, a young, attractive and prominent young woman in that bungalow out in the country there, on her own ...'

Angel reached out for the phone, pressed a button and said, 'Ahmed. Phone Scrivens and tell him I want to see him before he goes home tonight.'

'Right sir.'

He replaced the phone and turned back to Mac. 'Scrivens lives only two miles away from her. I'll get him to check on a few things, discreetly, on his way home.'

Angel rubbed his face and then his neck. He looked like an undertaker who had just made a refund.

Mac watched him. 'You are getting far too intense, Michael.'

'I should think so,' he snapped. 'I have that feeling the murderer is right under my nose …'

13

Ahmed opened the door. 'Miss Cumberland, sir.'

'Thank you for coming,' Angel said and pointed to the chair. 'Please sit down.' Ahmed went out and closed the door.

Kate Cumberland was a pretty young woman with a ready smile. She sat in the chair nearest the desk.

'Now then, I've asked you to call in to see me ... I didn't get the opportunity to have a word with you at the time your house was broken into. You've still no idea what the intruder was looking for?'

'No.'

'You were secretary to Lord Ogmore and worked up at the Hall until his death in June last year. Why did you leave?'

'I left because there was very little for me to do. When Lord Archie died, the bank called in the loan he had taken out to pay off the outstanding Inheritance Tax, which meant that the Hall would have to be sold. Her ladyship's situation was worsened by the rumour about the Ogmore diamond.'

'What rumour was that?'

'Well, Lord Archie used to keep this huge diamond in a little brown drawstring pouch in his pocket. He said it was safer and he wouldn't have to pay to insure it and comply with all the annoying conditions the insurance company

would have put on him. The rumour was that it didn't exist
… that it had been sold years back.'

'So, where is it now?'

'I suppose her ladyship has it. It was in his dressing-gown
pocket the day he died. I know because I saw it. Well, I saw
the pouch anyway. Only that morning he had had an earnest
conversation with Lady Emerald about something. The bills
and the bank loan, I believe. I didn't hear what was said
exactly. But he waved the pouch under her nose, I think to
reassure her that as long as he had the diamond, they would
be financially OK. I had heard him say that before.'

'Hmmm. And can you recall the day Lord Archie died?'

'I think so. He hadn't been well for about a week. Dr
Sinclair had been to see him a day or so before. I don't know
exactly what the trouble was. He did drink rather a lot. On
this particular day, he didn't get dressed, which was unusual.
He came into the drawing room in his pyjamas and dressing
gown, late. We went through the morning's post together.
There were one or two letters to see to, nothing much. Then
her ladyship came in. There was some query about a bill from
Heneberry's, the wine merchants. That's when he waved the
pouch in front of her. Next, Geoffrey Sanson came in with a
tray of tea, closely followed by Mrs Drabble who came in to
discuss the menu. As I recall, his lordship was sat on a big sofa
in front of the coffee table, where he'd seemed to enjoy a cup
of tea with Lady Emerald. But suddenly, his face changed.
He put the cup down, and asked her ladyship to send for Dr
Sinclair. She immediately rang through and he said he would
come at once. She lifted his feet and moved cushions around
him to make him more comfortable on the sofa. Then she
asked Geoffrey Sanson to push the sofa nearer the fire to keep
him warm, and she asked me to fetch a blanket from the
chest in the front hall, which I did. I helped her to cover him
with it. He looked very ill. He was perspiring and he lay there
with his eyes closed, but I don't think he was asleep. Mrs
Drabble cleared the tea things and came back with a cloth
and duster. She wiped the coffee table top and tidied up the

newspapers and things. Then we all left them together. That was the last I saw of him. Dr Sinclair arrived shortly afterwards. Geoffrey Sanson was hovering at the front door and showed him straight in, but I believe he had already gone.'

'Hmmm. And what happened to the diamond then?'

'Her ladyship would have taken it. It was hers by rights, of course. And it is immensely valuable.'

'Did anybody else know about the diamond?'

'Oh yes. Everybody knew about it.'

'Geoffrey Sanson played the role of butler very properly, you know. Like as if it was a part in a play. He wouldn't say anything out of turn, not to his lordship anyway. I think he always fancied himself as a lady's man. Perhaps he wouldn't have behaved so perfectly if, say, her ladyship had become a widow and he had been alive. Well, who wouldn't? With her looks and money and title?'

'Did he say so?'

'No, but you can work out what people are thinking if you watch them when they don't realize you are watching them, can't you?'

Angel nodded.

'And he was up to his eyes in debt, so Lord Archie strolling round the place with a diamond worth many millions in his pocket was like a red rag to a bull for him.'

'Oh,' Angel said. 'What was the reason for the debt?'

'Horses. Couldn't resist a gamble on the gee-gees, inspector. He used to boast about his winnings, but he never told us about his losses. There used to be a bookie on the phone to him regularly. I used to take the calls in the estate office, very roughly spoken man. Bertie or Bertram or some such name. Chasing him for money. He told me if ever he rung up I was to say he was out. He must have got himself into a right mess.'

'Did you know Mrs Drabble at all well?'

'Not really. She was a lovely lady. I can't imagine who would want to harm her. It's awful.'

'Mmmm. One last thing. In your travels, have you come across two tubby men in ponytails?'

'*Two?*' she smiled. She shook her head firmly. 'Not even one, inspector. They'd stick out like sore fingers. They wouldn't take any finding round here, would they?'

'No,' he lied.

*

The bungalow door opened.

'Good morning, Lady Ogmore,' Angel said. 'May I come in?'

'Of course,' her ladyship replied. She was dressed in a long dress that hugged her as if it had been sprayed on. Her hair was in perfect formation; her make-up could have been applied by Renoir. She pulled open the door further. 'Come on through, inspector. You've caught me dressed this time. And I see you've got rid of those crutches.'

'Not before time,' he replied, taking in a heady whiff of some expensive chemical out of a spray, as he squeezed between her and an armchair into the cluttered room.

She closed the door quickly, reached across to the armchair by the table, grabbed two thick magazines from the seat and a stocking draped over the back, and made them disappear. 'Please sit down, inspector. Excuse the mess. It's the maid's day off,' she said with a wry grin.

'Thank you,' he said, making himself comfortable. He then began rubbing the lobe of his ear between finger and thumb. 'I'm sorry to come unheralded. But I'm urgently trying to wrap this case up before the murderer visits anybody else.'

Her mouth dropped open; her big blue eyes stared at him. 'Oh yes,' she said breathily. 'Of course. The papers implied you weren't making much progress. Is that really true?'

'No. No,' he lied, loudly and magnificently. 'We have several lines of enquiry. But I want to ask you about the Ogmore diamond.'

'Yes?' she said, frowning. 'What about it, inspector?'

'What happened to it?'

157

'My dear father-in-law disposed of it, ages ago. Sold it to pay death duties, shortly after Archie and I were married. He jokingly used to say he had to sell it to pay for Archie's and my wedding reception. It would be about 1996 or even earlier than that.'

'Your husband's ex-secretary, Kate Cumberland, said that the day Archie died, she saw him wave a brown pouch containing the diamond in front of you. She had the distinct impression that he had it at that time and that you have it now.'

Lady Emerald's face tightened. 'If I had the diamond, inspector, do you think I'd be living in this squashed-up little place? The truth is that the only way my dear husband could keep the bailiffs at bay was by a show of financial strength, financial strength that we didn't have. It's amazing what impressionable snobs there are out there. Regrettably it all fell apart when he died. I hadn't the guile to perpetuate the myth ... and so I finished up here.'

'There wasn't a brown pouch then?'

'There was a brown pouch all right, inspector. But there wasn't a diamond in it.'

Angel nodded his understanding.

'Just one more thing, your ladyship. Do you know anything about two fat men with ponytails? Apparently well dressed ... in an expensive car.'

'No.'

The answer didn't surprise him at all. 'One last question: did you know that Geoffrey Sanson was in debt?'

'It would be the gee-gees. Yes, I knew about that. He tapped my husband a couple of times for a few hundred pounds. But he always paid him back. It wasn't for a big amount, was it? I'd hate to think ...' She stopped speaking and shook her head slightly.

'I don't know. I hope to find out all about that very soon.'

'Sanson was a nice man,' she smiled again. Her eyes looked distant as she recalled happy times.

Angel noticed a dimple form in her left cheek when she smiled. 'I understand that he liked you.'

'Yes. Yes … I believe he did … A nice man,' she said distantly.

'Yes.' Angel stood up. 'Well, thank you very much, your ladyship. That's all I need for now. I might want a statement about Geoffrey Sanson, if you wouldn't mind. Perhaps, also, you wouldn't mind coming to the station, sometime. You can give it to my sergeant. I'll give you a ring. Save time.'

'Of course. Of course,' she said crossing to the door. 'Anything I can do to help,' she added with a polite smile.

They shook hands. She opened the door. Angel hesitated on the step.

'May I have a look round the garden before I go? Your spring flowers … budding: I am a keen gardener.'

'Yes of course. There's not much to see, inspector. I haven't done a thing out there since I arrived.'

'Thank you,' he said. 'Goodbye.'

The door closed.

He turned away and strode down the short path to the L-shaped lawn and surrounding border. He stepped on to the middle of the lawn and looked closely at the turf; it was in need of cutting. Crossing to the borders farthest from the bungalow, he looked down at the dead tulips and daffodils and the dandelions, plantain and dock leaves beginning to show. He had seen what he wanted to see. Straightening up, he briskly returned to his car and made his way back to the station.

*

'Mrs Buller-Price called in to see you, sir,' Ahmed said.

Angel took off his coat and threw it at him. 'Oh yes,' he said vaguely. His mind was elsewhere.

'She left a message.'

Angel crossed to the desk and dropped into the swivel chair. 'What is it?'

'She remembered the name of the little girl who was the daughter of Cyril Sagar and his wife.'

Angel looked up at him. 'And what is it?'

'Elspeth, sir,' he said. 'Elspeth.'

Angel's eyes opened wide. 'Yes. That's it! I remember. I knew it was something daft. Elspeth Sagar. Yes. Now *that's* the woman I want you to find. She'll probably be married by now.'

'Right, sir. There was something else. Mrs Buller-Price is still expecting you for a cup of tea, sir.'

'Aye. Thank you, lad. Any other messages?'

'Dr Mac came in and left a file. It's on your desk. He said it was the PMs on Dr Sinclair and his wife. He said to tell you, he didn't think it contained anything you didn't already know.'

'Hmmm,' Angel groaned. 'Anything else?'

'You asked me to find Geoffrey Sanson's next of kin. I can't find any living relative, sir.'

'Hmmm. Right, lad. We'll have to give that one up. While I remember, there's some aerosols of paint in the stores. They were confiscated from that graffiti idiot who got a six-month ASBO. Tell the sergeant you want to borrow a couple for me. If there's a choice of colours, choose light ones, like white or yellow, but any will do. All right?'

Ahmed nodded and made for the door.

'And I want a hammer. A heavy one.'

He blinked. 'Right sir.'

'Are you going to remember all this, lad?' he snapped.

'Yes sir.'

'Mmmm. Right. And I nearly forgot. I want a moustache.'

Ahmed's eyes nearly dropped out. 'A *moustache*, sir? A *moustache*? Now where am I going to get a moustache from?'

'Oh, don't be such a defeatist, lad. And it has got to be *this* colour,' he said twitching his hair between his fingers. 'Get a big one. I'll cut it down to the size I want myself.'

Angel watched the door as it closed and smiled briefly. Then he leaned back in the chair and looked up at the ceiling.

The good humour left him. Giving out a long sigh, he rubbed his chin hard several times, then reached forward and picked up the phone.

He tapped in a number and waited. At length it was answered.

Angel said, 'Hello. Is that Mr Mountjoy?'

'Speaking.'

'This is Inspector Angel, Bromersley Police. I wonder if you could get to the station tomorrow morning, Mr Mountjoy. It's a matter of identifying the murderer.'

14

It was Friday, the thirteenth.

Angel picked up the plastic bag of bits and pieces he had asked Ahmed to procure for him and came out of the station by the rear door. He got into his car and drove out of the yard, turned into the road towards Huddersfield and along to Victoria Falls roundabout. Turning left up the road towards Barnsley for 200 yards, he stopped, turned round, parked up at the side of the kerb and got out his mobile. He tapped in a number.

There was a short wait, then a click and a woman's voice said, 'Hello?'

'Ah, good morning, Lady Ogmore. DI Angel here. I wonder if you'd be so kind as to call into the station and give my sergeant that statement about Geoffrey Sanson and what you knew of his financial situation, as we discussed?'

'Good morning, inspector,' she said brightly. 'Yes, of course. When would you like me to come?'

Angel smiled. 'Well, to suit you really. *Now*, would be *very* convenient?' he said hopefully.

There was a slight pause. 'I'll come straightaway.'

Angel beamed. 'Thank you so much. Ask for detective sergeant Gawber. He'll be expecting you. Goodbye.'

'Goodbye inspector.'

He nodded, pressed the button and tapped in another number.

It was promptly answered. 'Gawber.'

'She's on her way,' Angel said grimly.

'Right sir,' he replied.

Angel cancelled the mobile and dropped it into his pocket. He looked at his watch. He reckoned it would only take a couple of minutes for her ladyship to lock up the bungalow, get in her car, drive through the estate gates and down to Victoria Falls on her way to the station. He had the roundabout well in his sights; all he had to do was to wait.

Two minutes and forty seconds later, he saw the open-top white Porsche glide past the end of the road and round the island on its way to Bromersley. He nodded approvingly, started up the car engine, drove back to the roundabout, turned left along the main Huddersfield road for a hundred yards and left through the estate gates. Pulling up outside Lady Ogmore's bungalow, he grabbed the plastic bag, got out of the car and strode purposefully through the front gate along the path, down the side to the rear of the building. He looked round at the shrubs and field beyond. There were no signs of life in any direction. He took out the aerosol can of unsightly yellow paint, shook it and sprayed the pane of glass that had been replaced only nine days earlier.

Ahmed had borrowed a hammer from the station maintenance man. Angel reached into the bag for it and lunged at the window. There was a loud crash as the glass broke and jagged pieces of the yellow-painted glass dropped on to the path at his feet and into the bedroom. He continued the bashing until the hole in the window was big enough to gain access.

*

Angel opened the door of the CID briefing room and looked inside. He was pleased it was unoccupied. There was a table at the front, near the door, with a pile of books on it and a telephone. The wall behind it was fitted with a blackboard. A third of the board was covered with notes and photographs of persons wanted or missing and there was a column of names written up in chalk. A big map of Bromersley and the surrounding district covered a side wall, and in the body of the room were five rows of chairs, six in a row.

Angel wrinkled his nose: there was an unpleasant smell of fish and chips. He crossed to the window, opened it, then he went back to the table, picked up the phone and tapped in a number.

There was a click and a voice said, 'Gawber.'

'I'm back. Wheel her into the briefing room,' he said sombrely.

There was a click. He replaced the phone, ambled thoughtfully across to the chairs and sat on one at the front.

After a few moments, he heard footsteps along the corridor and Lady Emerald's gentle voice. 'In here, sergeant?'

'Yes please, ma'am,' Gawber said, and he remained in the doorway.

Angel stood up.

She glided through the door all smiles, as beautiful and immaculate as ever. She spotted Angel and crossed towards him. 'There you are, inspector. The sergeant is looking after me wonderfully well. It's so interesting to see where you work and where it all happens.'

'Would you like to join me, your ladyship?' He said indicating the chair next to him.

There was a momentary look of confusion on her face. She glanced swiftly round,   hesitated, smiled and said, 'Er yes. Of course.'

WPC Leisha Baverstock appeared at the door. Gawber whispered something to her. She nodded and came into the room.

Lady Ogmore stared into her face and then at the uniform of the WPC for a second, and forced a smile.

'Good morning, Lady Ogmore,' Leisha said, confidently, and sat down in the chair two away from her.

Her ladyship nodded and smiled. Her eyes darted from one to the other, round the room and back to the WPC. The smile left her and her hand went thoughtfully to her mouth.

Angel nodded at Gawber who disappeared leaving the door open. He put his elbow on the back of the chair and turned to face her. 'I have just returned from your bungalow, Lady Ogmore,' he began quietly. 'I am afraid I found it necessary to smash the glass in your bedroom window.'

Her mouth dropped open and she blinked several times.

'But I've sent a police constable and a glazier up there. It will soon be repaired again.'

She shrugged and said, 'Well, never mind, inspector. Accidents will happen.'

'Oh no. No,' he said quickly. 'It wasn't an accident. I did it on purpose.'

She shook her head very slightly. 'Well, it doesn't matter. If it's being repaired ...'

'Oh but it does, Lady Ogmore. It does. You see, although it may seem a detail to you, when you smashed the window nine days ago, fragments of glass flew all over the place ... on to the lawn ... even on to the border by the fence, twelve feet away.'

Her face went pale. Her eyes froze. 'I didn't smash any window.'

Angel held up a steadying hand. 'Now if it had been smashed from the *outside*, as I did this morning, most of the glass would have dropped on to the path and into the room on to your bedroom carpet.'

Gawber came back into the room and sat quietly next to him.

She hesitated. 'Not necessarily,' she said. 'It could have been windy.'

'It was a very calm and sunny day. I've just completed the experiment and the point is proven. I even painted the glass yellow so that it is easy to see it and it will not be confused with the glass fragments that spread further afield when you smashed it from the inside, as only you could have done.'

He waited.

Her mouth twitched, then she said: 'Don't be so ridiculous. Why would I smash my own window? It's preposterous.'

Angel pursed his lips. 'It's not that preposterous ... not when you wanted everybody to believe that you too were a potential victim.'

'This is nonsense. Not only is this ridiculous, but I know that you have to have proof. And *that* you can't have.'

'Oh but I do,' he said confidently. 'I've got an eye witness.'

'You can't have!'

'I have a witness who saw you leaving Alison Drabble's flat in your car in great haste, minutes after you had murdered her.'

'Ridiculous,' she said, her voice trembling. 'I was nowhere near her place the day she was murdered.'

'Ah. This man knows differently.' He glanced back over his shoulder at Gawber and nodded.

Gawber got up and went out through the door into the corridor.

Nobody spoke.

By now Lady Ogmore was red in the face, her breathing was heavy and unsteady, her hands shook at times but her jaw was set defiantly.

Angel licked his lips and rubbed his chin. He was trying to remain confident. It wasn't easy: he was depending upon an eye *witness who couldn't see*!

Gawber came back into the room leaving the door open. They exchanged glances as he returned to his seat next to Angel.

Lady Ogmore looked from one to the other and said, 'What's happening?'

'All will be revealed, your ladyship.'

After a few seconds, in the silence, they could hear the regular tapping of a stick against the wall along the corridor and a man with a moustache, dark glasses, in a light rain-coat and hat with a cream Labrador in its yellow dayglo and aluminium harness appeared framed in the doorway twenty feet away.

'Ah,' Angel called. 'Come in, Mr Mount joy.' The man gripped the aluminium harness tightly in his left hand and the white stick in his right and followed the dog a few paces into the room.

Her ladyship's mouth dropped open. She began to speak but stopped.

Angel called. 'Do you recognize this lady?'

'Yes,' he said confidently. 'She's the one I saw last Tuesday at about two minutes past two coming out of the recreation ground opposite Mrs Drabble's flat on Carlton Road. Nearly knocked me down. Kept pipping her horn. She could see I had a dog.'

Lady Emerald's face went scarlet. Her hands trembled. She licked her lips and swallowed. 'Ridiculous. He *couldn't* have seen me.'

'Come in. Sit down, Mr Mountjoy,' Angel said.

The man followed the dog to the table by the door. He carefully put his stick across the table top, let go of the harness, pulled out the chair behind the table and sat down. He touched the dog on its back and the animal gave a quick wag of its tail and flopped on to the floor by his side.

Lady Emerald followed the man's every move: her eyes were transfixed on him. 'It's a trick!' she shouted. Her hands were shaking. 'He *couldn't* have seen me.'

Angel sat there expressionless.

'Get him to *read* something,' she called.

Angel blinked and rubbed his chin.

'If he can see, get him to read something,' her ladyship said angrily.

Angel looked at Mr Mountjoy, pursed his lips and made a pleading gesture with his hands.

The man eventually said, 'What do you want me to read?'

Her ladyship's face contorted with anger and she said, 'Those books on the table. Take the third one down, and read aloud from that.'

He selected the third book down out of the pile of five and opened it at random. 'Shall I start from the top?'

'No!' she bawled angrily. 'Start at the second paragraph down?'

He held the book about fifteen inches from his face and, although he was still wearing sunglasses, he began to read, clearly and effortlessly. 'When the Police and Criminal Evidence Act 1984 came into force — on 1 January 1986 — police were given the power to photograph and fingerprint persons reported or charged with a recordable offence.' He stopped, lowered the book, looked up and said, 'Do you want me to go on?'

Angel looked at Lady Ogmore.

'That's not what's written,' she cried. 'He's remembered it from somewhere. It's a trick. I know it is. He *couldn't* have seen me!'

Angel nodded at Gawber, who went over to the man at the table, took the book from him and showed the open page to her. She hardly glanced at it. She wouldn't have been able to see it through all the rage and tears.

'Is it the second paragraph down?' Angel asked.

Gawber looked at the page then back at Angel and nodded. 'Yes.'

Angel turned back to Lady Ogmore.

'You're surely not suggesting he memorized all that stuff in all five volumes, are you?'

'I *thought* he was blind. I was *certain* he must be blind. Do you think I would have let a blind man stop me?' She shook her head several times and stared at the floor. 'I don't know what Archie did with it. It wasn't my fault he died and left all those debts,' she muttered. 'I couldn't stand to be poor again ... not at my age!'

Angel nodded. That was it. The game was up. He sighed, rose to his feet and turned to WPC Baverstock.

'You'd better search her first. I suspect she'll have a stiletto on her somewhere. *Be very careful.*'

Lady Ogmore's head had dropped on to her chest; her eyes were closed. She seemed to have fainted. Baverstock and Gawber took her by the arms and lifted her to her feet. Her handbag dropped to the floor and fell open. A powder compact, a small perfume aerosol and a silver-handled stiletto in a slim leather sheath slithered on to the parquet floor.

*

'Her fingerprints were all over it, sir,' Gawber said sombrely as he closed the office door.

'Aye,' Angel said, looking up from his desk and wrinkling his nose. 'Label it and put it with the other four. Have you charged her?'

'Yes sir.'

'Any drugs on her?'

'No. I've organized the MO to have a look at her. And phoned her solicitor. And Leisha — WPC Baverstock — has just taken her a cup of tea.'

Angel nodded and sniffed. 'Right. Have the doc check her thoroughly for needle marks. She couldn't have stuck knives into people without being hyped up with something. Or she's a much harder bitch than she looks. She would have had to get the stuff from either a bent doctor, a drug dealer or a booze shop. There's no evidence she takes drugs or drinks to excess! And where did she dump the empties or the syringes? I've had Scrivens go through her bins secretly the past few nights and there was nothing!'

'Her clothes would have been stained. Where did she dump the dresses? And she wore gloves, didn't she? Where are those?'

'We've got to find them, but what's more important is finding that diamond.'

Gawber blinked. 'Where do we start?' Angel rubbed his chin. 'Where she left off. Sit down a minute,' he said pointing to the chair. 'The last time the diamond was seen was the day Lord Archie died, and that was last June. It was in a brown pouch in his dressing-gown pocket, when Geoffrey Sanson, Kate Cumberland, Alison Drabble and Dr Sinclair were trotting in and out of the drawing room at Ogmore Hall for different reasons. It went missing from that room just before, or just after, his death. One has to assume that somebody stole it, or took it. But who? Or, in his dying moments, did his lordship give it to one of them for some reason for safe-keeping? If he did, why didn't he give it to his wife? Clearly he didn't or we wouldn't have had all this mayhem. We need to recover the diamond to complete the case against her. After all, *that* was the motive. She was left with a mountain of bills; the diamond, which was legally hers, would have removed all her money problems.'

'Will the case against her hold together if we *don't* find the diamond, sir?'

'That's the problem, Ron. I haven't any actual hard evidence. Just circumstantial clues. But I had to get her arrested as soon as I knew it was her, before she took it into her mind to murder somebody else. But I haven't got everything sewn up, far from it. It was only after I discovered glass on her lawn ... up to twenty feet away from the window, that I suddenly considered the possibility that she might have faked the break-in at her own bungalow. I experimented breaking the bungalow window from the outside, and the glass, of course, fell on to the path or went into the bedroom. That convinced me that the window had been smashed from the inside. It could only have been her. And then all sorts of possibilities became options. Matters I hadn't considered before, because I had thought she was a potential victim herself, came to mind and all the little discrepancies in her words and actions took on an ominous significance.'

'Such as what, sir?'

'Well, for example, Mrs Sinclair's body was slumped close to the French windows where the murderer left the house. At first, I thought it would have to be somebody strong to push against the weight of the dead body to get out. It takes a lot of effort to shift a corpse slumped on the floor like that. But then I realized it wouldn't have to be moved at all if the murderer was really slim, and *nobody's* slimmer than Lady Emerald!'

Gawber smiled grimly.

'She lied about the whereabouts of the diamond,' Angel continued. 'She said her father-in-law had disposed of it in his lifetime. But it was shown with her and her late husband in a photograph on the wall of her bungalow taken at a jewellery fair in 2000, which was the year *after* the old lord, Lord Lionel Ogmore, had died! There were other photographs on the wall that caught my attention. One was of her appearing as Juliet in Shakespeare's *Romeo and Juliet*, where she might have got the idea that it was easy to slip a dagger between somebody's ribs to kill them. And there was also her outstanding ability as an actress. She had had professional training and there was one photo that showed she had won a nomination for some big national acting award. She certainly played the real-life part of the sweet, harmless young widow struggling to keep up appearances, with aplomb. Also, when I visited Kate Cumberland's house, I saw an envelope postmarked 3 May from her that indicated she knew exactly where Kate was living, when only the day previously, the day she had posted the letter, she had told me that she had no idea where Kate lived. I now realize she deliberately concealed the address from me, so that she could break into the house and search for the diamond, before I could get there.'

Gawber shook his head. 'I never noticed any of these things.'

Angel smiled. 'You would if you were in my shoes. Anyway, lastly, the four stilettos used in the murders were presumed to be part of a presentation set of six. I recognized the design engraved on the handles, a sword and a snake topped by a lion's head, the same as that on the plaques over Victoria Falls, which were, of course, representations of the Ogmore coat of arms. And *that* discovery gave me a clue to the *source* of the stilettos. I still need confirmation. I think the tea set that Mrs Buller-Price bought at the auction from the Ogmore estate may be decorated with the same design and I need to check that out. I am going up there next week. Dear Mrs Buller-Price has been inviting me to tea for ages.'

'Mmmm. So where do we go from here, sir?'

'Well, I suppose Lady Ogmore was in the best position to know where the diamond was likely to be, and she thought it was in the possession of one of the four who visited her husband in the drawing room the morning he died. We'll simply have to go back over Sanson's, Drabble's, Kate Cumberland's and Sinclair's homes and start taking up the floorboards. It's got to be found, Ron. Wherever it is.'

There was a knock at the door.

'Come in,' Angel snapped.

The door opened. It was Ahmed. He glanced at the sergeant and then at the inspector and his jaw dropped. 'Oh,' he stammered.

'What is it, lad?' Angel growled.

'I thought you were on your own, sir,' he said, licking his lips nervously.

'What do you want? We are *all* ears,' he snapped.

'Well, sir, Leisha Baverstock said that Mr Mountjoy — the blind man — read a piece in the briefing room from one of those books on Police Rules and Regulations. And that that resulted in an admission of guilt by Lady Ogmore, and that she's been charged with the serial murders.'

'Yes lad, that's right.'

'Well, sir,' he said, looking down at his feet. 'I just wanted to ask you, how was it possible that Mr Mountjoy could do that? I mean, he's *blind!*'

Angel sighed. 'Oh is *that* all? Well, I can't be bothered with that now, lad. You work it out. And meanwhile I want you to find the whereabouts of Elspeth Sagar.'

15

It was Saturday: normally a day of relaxation and restoration for Michael Angel. The day he might have been in his old corduroys, cutting the lawn, weeding the borders, dead-heading the roses or repointing the patio. He might even have been helping Mary choose groceries and pushing a trolley round Tesco's, but this Saturday was different. He was in his best suit, collar and tie tootling round the side streets of Bromersley in his car.

Reaching one particular street, he put his foot on the brake and looked up at the sign on the corner of a house. It was Bartholomew Street. That was the one! He nodded approvingly. He let in the clutch and edged the car along until he saw the number eleven made up of chromium figures screwed on to a gate. That was the last known address he had for Mrs Sagar, Cyril Sagar's widow, and their daughter, Elspeth. He drove slowly past the house to the end of the short street, turned the corner and parked. Then he walked purposefully back to number eleven, went through the gate to the front door, pressed the illuminated bell push and waited. He didn't quite know what to expect. It was soon answered by a middle-aged toothy lady wearing a bright apron over an ill-fitting dress.

'Ye-eeess,' she said, her eyes looking decidedly suspicious and scanning him from his polished shoes to his smartly brushed hair.

Angel put on his best Roger Moore smile and said, 'Good morning. I'm from Imperial Television. I have some very good news for you. If your name begins with S, and you can give me the answer to the question posed on Channel 600, you have won the ten-thousand pound prize!'

The wariness left her. Her eyes shone with curiosity and interest. She came out on to the step, wiped her hands down her apron and said, 'What's this?'

Angel smiled at her. 'Does your name begin with the letter S, madam?'

'Yes.'

'Ah,' he said. 'And do you have the answer to the question?'

'What is the question?' she asked shrewdly.

'You need to be watching Channel 600, madam. That's the whole point of the game,' Angel said.

'Oh. Sorry. I haven't heard anything about it.'

Angel pulled out his notebook. 'Well, I'm sorry too. Because it means you haven't won the star prize. However, because you answered the door, you go into the draw for a consolation prize.'

'Oh?' she said, smiling eagerly.

He pulled out a notebook and pen. 'What is your name?'

'Stevens. Mrs Helen Stevens,' she said, her eyes twinkling with anticipation.

He wrote it down carefully. 'And this address is 11 Bartholomew Street. Hmmm. Now according to the information on our prize headquarter computer, there should be somebody living here called Sagar. If you can direct me to him or her, you may be eligible for our special super 'finders' conditional prize which, if you win, will entitle you to a weekend for two with Champagne and chocolates.'

'Ah,' she said. 'No. A Mrs Sagar did live here but she died last year and we bought the house from her daughter. Do you think that would count?'

'According to the rules, the daughter *would* be eligible to enter the contest but, of course, she would need to answer the question correctly. You only have to be able to direct me to the daughter and your name and address would go into the draw for a 'finders' star prize!'

'Wow,' she said. 'A star prize.'

'Does the lady's name begin with the letter E?'

'My husband's does,' she said enthusiastically. 'It's Eric. E for Eric.'

'I'm sorry. That doesn't count. But remember, you are already going into the draw for the weekend with Champagne and chocolates. Now, does the daughter of the lady who lived here before you have a name beginning with E?'

'Oh. I don't know. Why, yes. I think it was Elspeth. Yes.'

Angel smiled. 'If I can locate her, you've won the 'finders' prize. Now what is her full name and address?'

'Oh what have I won?'

'It's a three-star prize. I don't know exactly. Imperial Television will be contacting you. What is the lady's name and address?'

'It's Elspeth Gorman. I don't know the address, but it's one of those big, lumbering houses on the main road down to the Middlemass supermarket, somewhere opposite the wine shop. Have you any idea when they'll deliver it?'

The name 'Gorman' hit him between the eyes. That was Elspeth Sagar's married name. Where had he heard that name before?

... Quite recently, he was sure. The old photographer! Of course. He knew the houses she referred to. He turned away from the door.

She called after him. 'Will they deliver it soon?'

'Yes,' he replied. 'I'm sure they'll contact you first,' he added, edging away from her. 'Thank you very much. I should go back to the television now, Mrs Stevens. Keep watching the channel. There'll be more prizes!'

'Oh yes,' she whooped and closed the door.

Angel was soon on the main road into town and looking up at the big, lumbering houses as he drove slowly past them. There were four. It was a question of elimination. Each had its own dozen or so steps leading from a gate near the pavement up to the front door. A window at 90 degrees at the top of the steps meant that visitors could be observed and approved by the occupier before opening the door. That didn't aid Angel's situation. He needed to know which house was Elspeth Gorman's without her realizing she was being clocked. Driving past the houses to the roundabout, he made a 360-degrees turn and came back up the road, past them again, drove on another 100 yards and then parked. When he got out of the car he noticed he had parked outside a small branch of the Bromersley Building Society. He slipped into the office. At a ledge screwed to the wall desk, where you might sign a cheque or make out a deposit slip, were little boxes stuffed with leaflets offering different rates of investments and banking services. He dived into the nearest, picked up a handful and came out. Then he walked briskly down the street to the nearest of the four houses and ran up the steps. There was no sign of life. He glanced through the window by the door but saw nothing of interest. Pushing one of the leaflets through the letterbox, he came down to the pavement and repeated the action for the next two houses without success. At the fourth house, when he arrived at the top of the steps and glanced quickly through the window, he saw something that made his pulse race. Hanging in the window was a bright pink fluffy animal. It was an elephant or a pony, just as described by Mrs Buller-Price. There was no wonder she recalled it. The colour was so bright and bizarre it could only have originated from a far eastern country. That house was undoubtedly the home of Mrs Elspeth Gorman.

If Angel had had a tail, it would have been wagging.

*

It was 8.28 a.m. on Monday, 16 May, when Angel walked into his office. His phone was already ringing. He glared at it, reached over the desk and picked it up.

'Angel.'

It was Superintendent Harker. 'Ah, *there* you are,' he bawled. 'I want you down here, *now!*'

There was a deafening click before the line went dead.

Angel's eyebrows shot up. He replaced the phone and sighed. He wondered why Harker sounded more uncivilized than usual. Why did he have to make first thing on a Monday morning more miserable than it already was? He went straight out of the office down the green corridor and knocked on his door.

'Come in. What's all this about Lady Ogmore?' he bawled, his eyebrows bouncing up and down the front of his turnip-shaped head. 'I was away all weekend. This is the first I've heard of it,' he shouted.

'She's charged with murder, sir. She's on remand at Wakefield.'

'Murder?' he squawked. '*Murder!* I hope you know what you're doing, lad. Whose murder?'

'Sanson, Drabble and the two Sinclairs, sir.'

'Ridiculous! A nice young woman like that! Married into the leading family in the town. Her in-laws have given us Jubilee Park, the public library, Victoria Falls and I don't know what else. I hope you've got your facts right, lad. What's the motive, then?'

'The Ogmore diamond.'

'The Ogmore diamond? I thought that had been sold years back.' He shook his head and ground his teeth. 'Well, it belongs to her anyway, doesn't it? She'd inherited it.'

Angel stood there. There wasn't much point in saying anything. Whatever he said would be wrong.

'Well, what have you done with it? Supposed to be worth millions, isn't it? Put it somewhere safe, I hope. The bank would be the best place. We don't want it here. This station is full of bloody thieves!'

'We haven't actually got it yet, sir.'

'What!!' he exploded. 'Well, where is it?'

'I don't know.'

The superintendent's eyes nearly popped out of his head. 'How have you managed to construct a case, then?'

'It was difficult, sir. I *do* need to find it. I am about to instigate a thorough search, and demolition if needs be, of the victims' homes and Kate Cumberland's cottage and Lady Ogmore's bungalow, if necessary. I'll have to start on Geoffrey Sanson's house —'

'You can't do that! You're talking about more than a million pounds. It's not coming out of our budget and the Home office would never cover it.' He shook his head and continued grinding his teeth. Sniffing he said, 'Have you got any witnesses? Have you got anyone who actually saw Lady Ogmore stick the stiletto into one of the victims?'

'Not exactly, sir. No.'

'What's that mean?'

'I've got a witness who was outside the scene of the crime at the critical time.'

'Oh good. Who was that?'

'I told you about him, sir. Mr Mountjoy.'

'Mountjoy? Mountjoy? It rings a bell,' he said thoughtfully. Then his mouth opened and his jaw dropped. 'Not the *blind man*!?' he bellowed.

'Well, yes sir …'

The superintendent looked as if he was about to throw up. 'I think you've gone absolutely off your trolley, lad. I really do! A blind man as an eye witness? We'll be the laughing stock of all forty-three forces.'

The phone rang. The super reached out for it.

'Harker … Yes sir … Rightaway, sir.' He replaced the phone.

'I've got to go. I'll be away all day with the chief. You'd better think this all out again. I only hope to god you can make the case stick!'

Angel came out of the office. He was glad to leave. It was going to be a great week! He charged up to his own office, went in and closed the door. Dropping into the swivel chair he gazed up at the ceiling. There was no point in changing tack now. The case against Lady Ogmore had depended partly on her confession and partly on the proof of her motive. The CPS barrister had said that. So it would still hold together provided that he could produce the diamond …

There was a knock at the door.

'Come in.'

It was Ahmed with an armful of papers.

'I've got Dr Mac's report on Sinclair's house and your post, sir.'

Angel nodded towards the desk and Ahmed put the pile down.

The inspector felt in his coat pocket and pulled out a used envelope.

'I've got this address. It's the address of Elspeth Gorman. I want you to go to the town hall and discreetly look at the electoral roll, and find out who lives there with her, all right?'

'Right, sir,' Ahmed said as he took the envelope.

'Then I want you to contact the phone company, find out her number … it's probably in the book, anyway … and see who she phones and then check them out. I expect they'll mostly be to Selina Bailey.'

'The medium?'

'The *fake* medium!'

'Right, sir,' he said with a grin. Ahmed always liked work out of the office that he could do on his own, unsupervised.

'I'm out too. If you want me, you can get me on my mobile.'

Ten minutes later, Angel arrived in Temperance Yard, off a cobbled alley between two big shops on the main street in the town centre. He parked outside an open door with a big sign over it that read, 'Benny Peters & Son, Turf Accountants'. He put his 'Police' sign in the windscreen and locked the car. Then he walked up three steps and followed the painted arrow sign up the staircase. At the top, through a door, was a big smoke-filled room illuminated by four brightly lit, glittery chandeliers; a tannoy speaker was belting out odds, runners and prices in a distorted nasal monotone. Thirty or forty men were hanging around, looking at newspapers stuck on the wall or on their laps. At the end was a counter with a wire cage across the front of it. The men stared slyly at Angel. He guessed they had him pegged as a stranger; some may have deduced he was a police-man. They gave him furtive looks while shuffling and mutter-ing uneasily. He weaved his way through them to the counter and the wire cage at the end. A smart man in a jazzy waistcoat, a red bow tie and a miserable face stared at him guardedly.

Angel shoved his warrant card under the wire grille. 'Can I see Mr Peters, please?'

The man gawped at the warrant, then back at Angel. 'Yeah. Yeah. I'll get him.' His hand disappeared under the counter.

Angel knew it was to press a button.

The man pushed the warrant card back. Angel swept it up and put it in his pocket.

A bob hole in the wall behind the cashier opened. A man's bald head showed and a gruff voice said, 'What is it, John?'

The cashier leaned over and whispered something.

The bob hole snapped shut and four seconds later, the door next to it opened. A fat man in an expensive suit strut-ted through. He looked across at the policeman.

Angel could now see that the man had fancy-shaved facial hair, and what was more significant, he had a ponytail!

Angel blinked, then nodded with satisfaction. Maybe things in the detecting business were going to get better. He said nothing.

'Is this a raid?' Benny Peters asked quietly.

Angel shook his head. 'An inquiry.'

The man nodded then swivelled back a section of the grille, raised the counter top and opened a hinged gap in the counter. 'Come on through.'

Angel passed through the gap and followed him into the back office. It was just one small room with another fat man in shirtsleeves, seated at the table. The policeman immediately noted with great satisfaction that he also had fancy facial hair and a ponytail. This looked like the end of the trail for the two men with ponytails.

Benny Peters said, 'This is my son, Cecil.'

The second man was tapping figures from scraps of paper into an adding machine and pulling a handle.

'Police,' Benny said to his son. 'On an inquiry.'

Cecil looked up from the chore briefly, nodded, then carried on with the adding-up.

In front of him on the big table were scattered piles of papers, newspapers, ledgers, telephones and fish and chip wrappers.

Benny pointed to a stool and took one himself. 'Now what can I do for you, inspector? What are you enquiring about?'

Angel said, 'Geoffrey Sanson.'

Benny pulled a face. 'Geoffrey Sanson? Bad news. He's dead, isn't he?'

'Murdered.'

'I heard. That's eight hundred quid down the pan. I've crossed it off. We're moving on.'

'You were seen at an auction.'

'Yes. We were trying to catch up with him to pay what he owed us. We thought he'd be bound to be there. Lady do dah's auction. He used to work for her. We'd been looking for him for eight weeks. He kept saying he'd be getting some funds to pay us off, but he never did. He had arranged to meet us here, in this office, more than once. But he never showed.'

Angel pursed his lips and then said, 'At the post-mortem, he had some severe bruises on his stomach. Caused by being thumped with closed fists.'

Benny Peters said nothing. He just looked at him dead-pan and shrugged.

Angel continued: 'I've got a witness who saw you and Cecil up the ginnel, between the saleroom and the butcher's, punching him.'

Benny Peters licked his lips. 'He was a very smooth talker. He ran up a big bill with us. We gave him credit because we trusted him; he'd always paid up in the past. This time he didn't. He lied and he lied repeatedly. And when we asked to be paid, he became very arrogant and rude. We tried to get paid. That's all. My son might have got a bit excitable and impatient in response to his rudeness.'

'Do you deny you assaulted him?'

'Of course we do. He lashed out at me. My son was only protecting me.'

He stood there a moment and looked into Benny's face. The man didn't flinch. Angel rubbed his chin. This father and son would defend themselves vigorously against a charge of assault, and to be fair, the witness hadn't been near enough to see or overhear exactly what had happened. Also, he reckoned she wouldn't be assertive enough to make a powerful impression on a judge. This clearly wasn't a case to pursue.

Angel sniffed and said, 'Well take this as a warning then. In future, don't get so physical when collecting your debts.'

Benny Peters made an appealing gesture with his hands and face: words weren't necessary.

Angel wrinkled his nose. 'You didn't come across a diamond in your travels, did you?'

*

'Elspeth Gorman lives on her own at that address, sir. The phone company gave me the list of numbers she has called over the last month. There were only eight: all local, and I've checked them out. Four of those were made to the town hall. The others were to local shops, the *Bromersley Chronicle* and a doctor's surgery,' Ahmed said, looking up from his notes.

Angel rubbed his chin. 'No calls to that Selina Bailey?'

'No, sir.'

The inspector's face dropped. That was a blow. He had been relying on the list showing a link to the old woman. It would have been more than sufficient to show how the medium received her messages from the dead! In particular how she knew about his father and his great-aunt Kate. This was a great disappointment. He shook his head. Either the two women were smarter than he took them for, or he was up a gum tree. He sighed. How many ways, in this sophisticated age, can people communicate in secrecy? He suddenly had an idea. 'Is there an internet charge on her phone bill?'

'No, sir.'

'Mmmm. What about old lady Bailey?'

'No. She's not on the internet either.'

Angel rubbed the back of his neck. He had to know how these two women exchanged information. He was convinced that they were in cahoots. To do her medium trick, particularly in regard to knowing about his late father, Selina Bailey would need communication with someone who had access to recent local history, particularly the dead. This problem was going to need his direct personal action.

'Right,' he suddenly said decisively. 'Ahmed, I want you to go down to the stores. They're always chucking out cardboard boxes. I want you to get me a big one ... a really big one.'

Ahmed gawped at him. 'How big, sir? What are you going to put inside it?'

*

Angel stopped his car outside Elspeth Gorman's house. He pulled on the handbrake, took out his mobile and, consulting an envelope from his pocket, tapped in a number. This was the one occasion in his life he hoped *not* to get a reply. He let it ring a few minutes until he was satisfied the woman wasn't at home. Then he cancelled the call, let in the clutch and drove the car round the block, out of sight of the house, and parked. He took a clipboard and an enormous cardboard box out of the car boot, and walked back round the corner to the bottom of the steep steps that led up to Elspeth Gorman's front door. After plonking the box on the pavement, he began to make a conspicuous and noisy ascent up the steep steps.

Although the box was empty, he heaved and groaned and slowly took it up the twenty or so steps, a step at a time, making as much of a show as he could. By the time he had arrived at Elspeth Gorman's front door and pressed the bell, the next-door neighbour was hanging out of her front window.

'She's out. There's nobody in. She's out at work. Who did you want?' the blousy woman called.

Angel looked down at the box and then at the clipboard, 'A Mrs Elspeth Gorman, love. Have I got the right house?'

'You've got the right house, but she's at work. She works at the town hall. They don't finish until half past five.'

Angel smiled. That was a great piece of free information. He noted it on the clipboard. He wondered what office she worked in.

'Oh,' he said. 'I thought they finished at five.'

'I don't know about other folk that work there, but she works in the Registrar's office, and they definitely don't finish until five-thirty.'

'Oh,' he nodded, and wrote *that* down with even more satisfaction. Great. So she worked in hatched, matched and despatched: couldn't be better placed to know who had died and who was related to whom, could she?

She pointed at the big box. 'Do you want me to take that in for her? I often do that. I don't know why I offer. She wouldn't do anything for me.'

Angel smiled at her. 'That's very kind. But unfortunately I can't. I have to ask her something before I can leave it.'

'Why? What is it? It looks heavy.'

'It's a computer. It's a prize.'

'Huh! She won't have time for that. With all her old photographs and stuff.'

He frowned. 'Photographs?'

'All that her father-in-law left. Old man Gorman. There's a mountain of old photographs of old Bromersley and all the old folks of fifty years ago holding those walls up. She's always up in that attic, messing about.'

The penny dropped. Angel remembered. Of course: Gordon Gorman, the old photographer who monopolized the studio work, passport pictures and the local weddings in Bromersley for over fifty years. Then he produced illustrated books on local history. He must have been her father-in-law. Hmmm. A valuable source of local information from yester-year: couldn't be better for her.

'She's hardly time to fit in her other business,' the old woman added raucously.

Angel smiled, hopeful of more information. 'Oh yes,' he said. 'And what's that?'

'Out nearly every night. Always after dark,' she said with a smirk.

Angel pursed his lips and looked at her with eyebrows raised. At length he shook his head.

'She must be on the game.'

With that she pulled in her head and slammed down the window.

*

'Ahmed. There you are, lad. Come in. I want you to get me a camera with a flash and a night sight from the stores. I want to take it home with me when I go.'

'Right sir,' Ahmed said and turned towards the office door to leave. He suddenly turned back. 'By the way, sir ...'

'Yes? What, lad?'

'You were going to tell me how Mr Mountjoy could see Lady Ogmore and everything ... and read from that book? I *know* he was blind because I showed him into your office last week, and he couldn't have managed without his stick and his dog.'

'It was a matter of bluff, Ahmed. Mr Mountjoy told me that the murderer must have seen him while he or she was leaving Alison Drabble's flat, because the car had braked hard close up to him and because of the insistent way the horn had been used. Therefore we knew the murderer, Lady Ogmore as it turned out, would have had a good look at him and naturally would have believed — because of the dog, the white stick and the tinted glasses — that he was blind. Now, her dress and her gloves would have been stained with blood at the time. Therefore, obviously, if she had thought that Mr Mountjoy could have seen her, and therefore subsequently identified her, she would most certainly have murdered him too, either then or later. So, when Mr Mountjoy went through that pantomime on Friday last and obviously *could* see — the realization and shock of the consequences were too much for her, and she gave herself away.'

'Yes, I understand that, sir. But what I don't understand is how did Mr Mountjoy suddenly regain his sight and was able to see?'

'Because it wasn't *the* Mr Mountjoy you had met. It was his brother, whose sight is perfect and he is of a similar build. What did you think I wanted the moustache for?'

Ahmed's jaw dropped.

16

'What's for tea? Is it nearly ready?' Angel said, pulling a bottle of German beer out of the fridge, shutting the door, presenting the bottle to the gadget on the wall and taking the cap off.

'It'll be ten minutes,' Mary said ushering him out of the kitchen into the hall.

He stood there and poured the cold beer slowly down the side of the glass like a professional bartender. Then he took a sip. 'I've got some news for you.'

'Oh,' she said lifting a pan lid and stabbing a simmering cauliflower with a fork. 'What's that?'

'I've found Cyril Sagar's daughter. Her name's Elspeth. She was married to Gordon Gorman's son.'

'Who's he?'

'The old photographer, who took the photos at mum and dad's wedding ... the ones with Aunt Kate ... with her stick.'

'Oh yes. I remember the name. We've got photos in our albums with his sticker on.' 'Yes. That's how *she* would know about Aunt Kate having a stick. Aunt Kate was in all our family photographs. She was never seen without her stick.'

Mary didn't say anything. She opened the oven, looked in it briefly, closed the door and altered the setting.

'What about *that* then,' Angel said triumphantly, sipping the beer.

'Mmmm.'

'She works in the town hall in the Registrar's office. Handy for knowing who has died, married or anything else to do with local family relationships, don't you think?'

He took another drink and waited, but Mary didn't say anything. She lifted the lid on the potatoes then put it back.

Angel said, 'Don't you see, I've found out who told Selina Bailey about this business between my dad and Cyril Sagar. It was Cyril Sagar's daughter, Elspeth Gorman.'

'So you say.'

'Well I was thinking. I vaguely remember my dad telling me how thirty-odd years ago, when he was a young copper on nights, he came across a crashed car stuck in the wall of a pub. In the driving seat was Cyril Sagar, drunk and incapable. Dad brought him home, and filled him up with coffee. Then took him to his own home, to his wife. As he sobered up, Cyril rang into the station and reported that his car had been stolen. But the pub landlord had already phoned in and said that he had seen Cyril Sagar run into his wall. He claimed it was in retaliation for him refusing to serve Sagar any more drink. CID were called to the car and took fingerprints and surveyed the scene. When Dad reported back at the station, the story about Cyril Sagar was on everybody's lips. This resulted in Sagar being charged and subsequently thrown out of the force. The rest you know. He jumped off a bridge across the Ml. His widow blamed Dad for betraying her husband. She said he could have covered it up. And she must have subsequently brainwashed her daughter into believing it. The coincidence of me coming to a Selina Bailey seance was an irresistible opportunity for her to vent her spleen.'

'You're saying this Elspeth Gorman regularly feeds information to Selina Bailey about her clients?'

'Yes.'

'And you've got proof of that, have you?'

'No. But I'm going to get it tonight.'

*

It was 9.30 p.m. and getting dark when Angel drove his car through Bromersley town centre to Anchor Road where Elspeth Gorman lived. He parked it fifty yards from her house opposite a small frontage of shops. Pulling on the handbrake, he took out his mobile, and tapped in a number. He put the phone to his ear and listened to it ringing out. After a few moments, there was a click and a strident woman's voice answered: 'Hello, yes?'

'Is that the Chinese takeaway?' he said, assuming a naive voice.

'No,' she said indignantly. 'This is a private number. This is 678423. You must have misdialled.'

'Sorry to have troubled you,' he said and stabbed the cancel button. She was still in the house; all he had to do was wait.

There wasn't much traffic about. He looked out at the quiet street; it was a secondary road, a mixture of small shops and houses. The shops were shuttered up and in darkness, while most of the houses had warm yellow light glowing through flowered curtains or cream-coloured blinds. The hardworking Bromersley public was settling in for an evening's relaxation. He sighed and wriggled lower into the driving seat, his eyes concentrating on Elspeth Gorman's side door. He didn't have to wait long. At five minutes to ten, the room light went out and seconds later a slim woman in an ocelot coat and wearing high heels appeared at the door. She skipped quickly down the steps to the street. Angel sat up. He was going to have to move swiftly to keep her in his sights. She turned down the street towards the roundabout and crossed the road. Angel leaped out of the car and set off fifty yards behind her. She turned up Jubilee Road, which led to Park Road. Angel crossed over so that he was on the opposite side of the road. The sky was as black as a witch's cat, but the streets were well lit with yellow halogen lights. At the end of the road, at the corner, she slowed down and looked back. He reduced his speed to a casual pace. She looked a wily bird. Her silhouette created by an amber street light showed she had a thick mop of hair, a stick-like figure and thin legs.

Park Road was a long straight road. It was going to be difficult to follow her clandestinely. She took the corner and Angel increased his speed to the junction, which took him ten seconds or so. By the time he had arrived there, she had disappeared. She must have gone down Park Road: there was no other way she could have gone. He pressed on down the road. At the other side he noticed a gap in the wall. It was an entrance to the park for pedestrians. Driving past in a car, you would hardly notice it. She must have left the road and entered the park there. Jubilee Park was not illuminated with street lights. Following Mrs Gorman in the dark was going to be tricky.

He crossed the road, turned through the gap in the wall on to the narrow path in the park. He could not hear or see any movement. He stood motionless in the middle of the path and listened. All he could hear was his heartbeat. It was louder than the drums at the Edinburgh Tattoo. A double-decker bus passed on the road behind him. The light from the upstairs windows briefly illuminated the path and he suddenly saw the outline of Mrs Gorman ahead of him. She was moving rapidly towards the Ogmore memorial. Angel decided it was too risky for him to follow her closely. His footsteps might be heard. He would approach it from a different direction. Stepping on to the grass, he ran along the turf to the bandstand to approach the Ogmore memorial from the far side. He saw her again in silhouette as a heavy vehicle on Park Road illuminated her briefly from the far side. She still appeared to be heading for the statue.

He moved down towards the memorial from behind, along a sweep of grass. He recalled that there was a bench in front of the statue where, at the height of summer, visitors sat and enjoyed the bank of flowers the parks department cultivated and planted out. He was fifty yards away now and could see the outline of his lordship standing on a plinth wearing a frock coat as solid as black bronze could make it. Tiptoeing very slowly, he measured every step before moving his body weight on to the next foot. He could hear whispering. Elspeth Gorman had obviously kept her nightly rendezvous with Selina Bailey. The two witches were sitting on the bench in front of the statue. He pulled the camera out of his pocket, removed the lens cap, pulled it up to his eye to rehearse the action then lowered it. He was all set, but he had to be certain to come upon them before they realized they were being observed. He was now near enough to hear earnest whispering including the eerie predominant whistle of the letter 's', but he could not make out any of the words. Slowly he closed in. He was only a few feet behind the plinth. Pulling the camera up to his face, he stepped forward and said, 'Good evening, ladies.'

There was a gasp. Both women turned towards him.

The camera flashed.

They leapt up from the bench.

The camera flashed again.

'Good evening. It's Detective Inspector Angel from Bromersley Police. Do you remember me?'

Neither replied.

The camera flashed again.

They upped and ran wildly and silently across the park like phantoms in the night. His jaw stiffened as he lowered the camera and rubbed his chin. He sighed as he remembered his father.

*

It was 8.28 a.m. the following morning, Tuesday, 17 May.

Ahmed closed the door.

Angel pointed to the camera. 'I took three photographs last night, lad. I think one will show the two women

191

distinctly. They are Selina Bailey and Elspeth Gorman. Will you print it off smartly for me?'

'Yes sir.'

'Off you go, then. Take the camera with you. Bring the snap in as soon as you've done it. Chop chop.'

Several minutes later, Ahmed appeared, carefully holding the colour print between thumb and forefinger. He placed it on Angel's desk. 'Careful, sir. The ink's still wet.'

Angel look down at the photograph and beamed. 'Ah! That's just what I wanted. Yes lad. I'll keep this. I want my wife to see it. *This* will surely convince her,' he said grandly.

Ahmed went out.

The rest of the morning passed with minimal interruptions and Angel had been able to reduce substantially the pile of papers on his desk. He looked up at the clock. It was 2 p.m. Leaning back in the chair, he rubbed his eyes. He felt the need for some fresh air. There were no appointments or commitments that afternoon, and he recalled his several promises to drop in on Mrs Buller-Price. Also, coincidentally, the CPS had been pressing him to check the engraving on the silver tea set she had bought at auction from the Ogmore estate. If the pattern matched that on the handles of the stilettos, it would strengthen the case against Lady Ogmore and would show the source of the murder weapons. Angel decided he could kill two birds with one stone: he could partake of a piece or two of her excellent Battenberg and check out the silver tea set at the same time.

He pushed away from the desk, put on his coat and made his way down the bottom corridor to the rear entrance. The air outside smelled good. Summer was on its way. He pulled the car away from the station and was soon on the Huddersfield Road out of   Bromersley. A little way along, he came to a stop. There was a traffic jam ahead. Nothing moved for half a minute, then the car in front edged forward and Angel engaged gear and let in the clutch. Selina Bailey's house was on the left and the reason for the hold-up appeared to be the presence of a removals van outside her house. As

Angel got nearer to it, he could see the old witch herself in the doorway, directing two men carrying a round dining table down the garden path towards the van. He slowed to observe as much as possible and saw a handmade poster in the downstairs window. It read: 'House for sale. Apply Wade and Son. Telephone 203760.'

Angel nodded with satisfaction, changed gear and sped away. He hoped that that was the last he would hear of Selina Bailey and Elspeth Gorman.

Soon he was approaching the hill down to the Victoria Falls roundabout. A sign in the road slowed him down: 'Slow — Workmen ahead.' He had not had notice of roadworks and had not heard of any RTAs, so he wondered what was ahead. As he reached the roundabout, he saw a red lorry with the words 'Bromersley Borough Council, Highways Department' painted on the cab door. The lorry was parked on the roundabout itself, next to the pool wall. There was no water spraying out of the fountain, but the road surface around was being washed by water about a quarter of an inch deep. Two men in dayglo yellow coats were fishing in the pool with long-handled nets. On the many occasions he had driven past the monument Angel had never known this happen before. He pulled on the handbrake, wound down the window and called across to them.

'I'm inspector Angel from Bromersley Police. What's the trouble?'

One of the men let go of his net and ambled across to the car window, pleased to have an excuse to break off. 'Somebody's bunged up the bottom of the pool with all sorts of junk,' he said grumpily. 'It's choked up the pump.'

'Oh?' Angel frowned.

The man pulled a miserable face. 'Yes. You wouldn't believe it. Dresses, skirts, gloves and bottles. Must have thrown them in the pool as they drove past ... as if it was a coconut shy.'

Angel's eyes glowed. 'Oh? Hmmm,' he said knowingly. 'Are those bottles vodka bottles by any chance?'

'Eh? I don't know. Just a minute,' the man said. He went over to the lorry and lifted a bottle out of the back and brought it across. It was a clear-glass bottle with a red and silver label stuck to it, which read, 'Minska. Pure vodka. Bottled in Warsaw. 1 litre.'

'I want you to save all that stuff for me? Bring it to the police station when you've done. Ask for DS Gawber.'

'Right, mate.'

Angel took off the handbrake and sailed up the hill and passed Ogmore Hall and Lady Emerald's bungalow without even a glance. He reached the signpost to Tunistone in about three minutes and continued on the main road towards Manchester. Two hundred yards later, he slowed down, turned hard right and pointed the bonnet up the steep single track towards the television mast on the top of the mountain. Halfway up was a wooden sign swinging at a tipsy angle, no doubt having recently suffered a blow from a 1986 Bentley. The sign read: 'Buller-Price Farm.' He turned through the open gate and travelled bumpily along an unmade track down the side of a field to another gate into a farmyard. There were three barns next to each other and the farmhouse beyond. He stopped the car at the front door of the house and got out. As he slammed the door five dogs came running from behind a barn barking and yapping and kicking up dust. They charged towards him, just as Mrs Buller-Price appeared wearing a big white apron over a voluminous brown coat and carrying a dangerous-looking hay rake. She looked anxiously at the car and then beamed with delight when she saw Angel standing beside it.

'Steady chaps. *Steady*,' she called. 'You remember Inspector Angel. He's a friend of ours. He's all right.'

The brindle Alsatian immediately returned to Mrs Buller-Price's side; the other four assorted mongrels slowed their gait and surrounded him wagging their tails and sniffing at his shoes and hands. He smiled down at them as he locked the car door.

She trundled up to him. 'There you are, inspector. At last. This is indeed a great pleasure. Come along into the house. I'll soon have the kettle on.'

'Thank you. I can't stay long, Mrs Buller-Price.'

She shook her head stubbornly, leaned the hay rake against the wisteria around the farmhouse door and went inside. Angel stooped slightly and followed her into the hall.

'I have been eager to christen my new silver tea service, and you'll be having a slice or two of my Battenberg,' she said firmly.

The dogs dashed in behind, piling on to each other in the scrum.

'You know your way. Do make yourself comfortable.'

Settling on the sitting-room floor, the dogs instantly pretended to be asleep.

'Sit down there, inspector,' she said, indicating a big easy chair facing the fireplace. 'Tony Curtis always sits there. What a day!'

She went into the kitchen.

Angel took the big chair and looked round the small sitting room, comfortably furnished with a huge old sideboard heaped with newspapers, letters and magazines. He could see *The Farmer's Weekly*, The *Pig Breeder's Gazette* and *Jersey Milk* spread untidily; also a pair of rubber gloves, a bottle of Black Rum and a glass. An assortment of large, easy chairs, each loaded with two or three cushions of various shapes and sizes, faced the big fireplace, which had a small fire glowing in it. Ten dusty-blue rosettes, as big as dinner plates and with '1st Prize' printed in the middle of each, hung limply from the mantelpiece. The room was untidy, dusty and warm, and he could smell cut flowers, dogs and freshly baked bread.

'It is nice to see you here at last, inspector,' she called from the kitchen. 'You come on a perfect day, although I have been very busy. I've never stopped and am quite ready for a sit-down. I was up at five, you know, and I had to milk my Jerseys, and roll the churn up the lane.'

She returned with a tray and put it on the table. 'There we are,' she said and flopped into the chair next to Angel.

Angel looked across at the three-piece silver tea service on the tray with great interest.

She noticed his attention.

'Yes inspector. This is the tea set I bought at the auction; the actual tea set given to Lord Arthur and Lady Alice Ogmore on their wedding day in 1842 by Queen Victoria and Prince Albert. It is a bit battered, but I have given it a thorough polish. It's come up well, hasn't it? I have been waiting for someone to call so that I could actually use it. I have had no one to share that pleasure with so far. I am so glad it's you.'

He noticed a small dent in the spout as he peered more closely at the chasing on the side of the teapot, the milk jug and the sugar basin. It was a long sword with a snake twined round it and a head of a lion at the top, the same emblem as on the stilettos and the plaques at Victoria Falls.

'It takes two and a half minutes to mash.'

He smiled at her agreeably.

There was a pause, then Mrs Buller-Price pressed her chins on to her chest and said, 'I heard on the radio that you've charged Lady Emerald with those horrible stabbings. That was a shock to the system, I can tell you. I suppose there's no possibility of a mistake, inspector?'

'Oh no. She's virtually admitted it.'

'Mmmm.'

'Do you believe, inspector, that the pot the tea is brewed in, affects the taste?'

'I certainly do,' he replied. 'This should have a very superior taste, shouldn't it?'

She looked at her watch. 'Ah. We shall see.' She picked up the teapot and tilted the long spout over her best Royal Doulton cups.

Angel looked on.

Nothing happened. Nothing came out. She tilted the teapot further. Still nothing happened. No tea appeared. 'Oh?' she said and looked across at Angel. Shaking the teapot vigorously, she then opened the lid and peered inside. 'Looks all right.'

'Hmmm. Try again.'

'Might be an air lock. Not been used for a year, you know.'

She tilted the teapot to an extreme angle; still no tea arrived.

Angel put down his plate. 'May I look?'

She handed it to him. He stood up and took it into the kitchen and up to the sink. He opened the teapot lid and peered inside. 'There must be a blockage. We will have to lose the tea, I'm afraid.'

Mrs Buller-Price came up behind him. 'Yes, of course.'

As he tipped up the teapot, the tea and teabags dropped into the bowl.

'I need something long and thin.'

Mrs Buller-Price rummaged in the sink unit drawer and offered him a long-handled wooden spoon. He looked at it, nodded approvingly and eased it down the spout. It met an obstacle about five inches down. He gave the spoon a smart tap with the palm of his hand and something gave way. Then he withdrew the spoon handle, turned the teapot upside down over the draining-board and shook it. A brown soggy dollop tippled out. It looked like a big teabag. Angel's jaw dropped as he looked down at the steaming lump.

'Whatever is it?' Mrs Buller-Price asked, her hand to her mouth.

'Scissors,' Angel said briskly.

She quickly found some and handed them to him.

He stabbed into the hot little pouch and made several snips to reveal a single, clear, glittering stone the size of a plum.

Mrs Buller-Price's eyes shone. Her hands went up in the air. 'It's the Ogmore diamond!' she whooped.

THE END

YORKSHIRE MURDER MYSTERIES

Book 1: THE MISSING NURSE
Book 2: THE MISSING WIFE
Book 3: THE MAN IN THE PINK SUIT
Book 4: THE MORALS OF A MURDERER
Book 5: THE AUCTION MURDERS

Don't miss the latest Roger Silverwood release, join our
mailing list:
www.joffebooks.com/contact

FREE KINDLE BOOKS

Please join our mailing list for free Kindle crime thriller, detective, mystery, romance books and new releases!
www.joffebooks.com

Thank you for reading this book. If you enjoyed it please leave feedback on Amazon, and if there is anything we missed or you have a question about then please get in touch. The author and publishing team appreciate your feedback and time reading this book.

Our email is office@joffebooks.com

Follow us on facebook www.facebook.com/joffebooks

We're very grateful to eagle-eyed readers who take the time to contact us. Please send any errors you find to corrections@joffebooks.com

CPSIA information can be obtained
at www.ICGtesting.com
Printed in the USA
FSHW011949260421
80876FS